Nancy Drew®
in
Password to Larkspur Lane

D1396207

Nancy Drew Mystery Stories® in Armada

For contractual reasons, Armada has been obliged to publish from No. 51 onwards before publishing Nos. 43–50. These missing numbers will be published as soon as possible.

Nancy Drew Mystery Stories®

Password to Larkspur Lane

Carolyn Keene

Armada

First published in the U.K. in 1971 by
William Collins Sons & Co. Ltd, London and Glasgow
First published in Armada in 1976

This impression 1988

Armada is an imprint of
the Children's Division, part of
the Collins Publishing Group,
8 Grafton Street, London W1X 3LA

Printed and bound in Great Britain by
William Collins Sons & Co. Ltd, Glasgow

"The blue flame again!" Mr Corning gasped

CONTENTS

Singing Horses

"IF this were two thousand years ago—!"

Nancy Drew paused on the flagstone path of her garden in front of a border of beautiful larkspur. For a moment the attractive red-haired girl of eighteen watched the tall blue plumes waving in the breeze. Then she turned to the middle-aged woman behind her.

"I must select the very best for the flower show, Hannah," she said.

The Drews' housekeeper and Nancy paused to look up at a passing aeroplane. They were startled to hear its engines cut out. As Nancy and Hannah watched in alarm, a wounded bird plummeted down and landed amongst the flowers.

"A homing pigeon!" Nancy exclaimed, seeing the tiny metal tube attached to its leg. "Maybe the bird's carrying a message!"

Hannah Gruen's eyes were on the plane. "Oh, Nancy!" she gasped. "It's going to crash!"

Nancy gazed upward and saw that the twin-engine craft was flying very low. The plane was tan colour and had a curious design outlined in black on the fuselage.

"It looks like a winged horse," Nancy thought, but

she could not be sure, since the sun was shining in her eyes.

Suddenly the coughing engines roared to life and the plane nosed upward, then zoomed away.

"Whew!" Hannah exclaimed. "I thought that thing was going to fall right onto our house!"

"I wonder if the plane hit this pigeon," Nancy said, and once more turned her attention to the bird, which was panting feebly.

"You poor dear!" she said, picking it up. Gently Nancy felt for broken bones, but found none. "The pigeon may only be stunned," she said.

"What a miracle that it's alive!" Hannah said.

Nancy nodded. "I'd better see if the pigeon's carrying a message. It might be something important that we ought to report to the bird's owner."

While the housekeeper held the pigeon, Nancy removed the top of the capsule on its leg and slid out a thin piece of paper. She unrolled the message and read aloud:

"*'Trouble here. After five o'clock blue bells will be singing horses. Come tonight.'*"

Nancy and Hannah looked at each other in puzzlement. "It's a strange message," the housekeeper said. "What in the world does that mean?"

"I wish I knew," Nancy replied, "but it sounds urgent—and mysterious." She slipped the message into her pocket. "I'll wire the International Federation of American Homing Pigeon Fanciers and give them the number stamped on the bird's leg ring. All homing pigeons are registered by number so the owners can be traced."

She examined the ring containing the digits 2-21-12-12,

then hurried off to phone the telegram. By the time she returned, Hannah had placed the bird in a cardboard box lined with cotton.

Nancy brought an eye-dropper and with it gave the pigeon water. Then she put some wild-bird seed in the box. "Do get well," she said softly.

"How are pigeons trained to carry messages?" Hannah asked as Nancy placed the box on a garage shelf.

"They have a home loft. No matter where the birds are released, they always fly back there."

"Did you ever hear how fast they can fly?"

"I read about some pigeons who raced from Mexico City to New York, averaging a mile a minute." Nancy glanced at her watch. "I'd better hurry or I won't get to the flower show on time."

She continued snipping prize larkspurs and putting them in a basket.

"Before all the excitement began," said Hannah, "you were saying, 'If this were two thousand years ago—,' but you didn't finish. What did you mean?"

Nancy smiled. "I was thinking that if I had lived two thousand years ago I might have been a Grecian maiden. And in that case, I might be praying right now in the Temple of Apollo at Delphi. I always imagine flowers there. Maybe delphinium—that's another name for larkspur."

"What would you be asking for?" said Hannah.

"That my father's olive groves would bear extra well, that his vines would be loaded with grapes and his nets heavy with fish every morning."

Hannah laughed heartily at the thought of her employer, Carson Drew, the well-known lawyer, picking olives or hauling in a fish-filled net.

While talking, Nancy and Hannah had been cutting stalks with the finest flowers and before long they had a basketful. Nancy took it into the kitchen and carefully fashioned an exquisite arrangement in an old English vase. She carried it to her convertible parked in the circular drive.

She thought, "My car was a good-looking one until that horrid man ran into it last week." Ruefully she surveyed the dent.

"Good luck with your entry," Mrs Gruen said. "Hope it wins a prize!"

"Hannah, you're a darling!" Nancy exclaimed and kissed her. The two had a deep affection for each other. The girl's mother had died when Nancy was very young and the housekeeper had helped Mr Drew bring up his only child.

As Nancy drove across the town of River Heights, she mulled over the strange message on the homing pigeon. Was it a code? Suddenly it occurred to Nancy that the pigeon might have been released from the plane which accidentally struck it. She wondered what the reply would be from the Homing Pigeon Fanciers association.

"Maybe," she thought excitedly, "I've stumbled upon a new mystery!"

By this time she had reached the Blenheim estate on the outskirts of River Heights. The broad tree-shadowed lawn was filled with women setting up displays for the annual charity flower show. Nancy had been assigned a spot in the greenhouse behind the mansion.

As she set her larkspur arrangement in place, the chairman came up to her. "My, Nancy, your delphiniums are gorgeous," Mrs Winsor said.

"Thank you," Nancy replied.

"I just adore larkspur," the woman said. "Such a lovely old-fashioned flower. My grandmother had them in her garden. She always had hollyhocks and bluebells, too."

Bluebells! Nancy's mind leaped to the mysterious message. Could the *blue bells* in it mean flowers?

Aloud she said, "Mrs Winsor, I hope the judges like my flowers as much as you do!"

Nancy hurried back to the convertible. She was eager to get home and see if a reply to her telegram had come.

To make better time, Nancy turned off the main highway on to a little-travelled shortcut. As she drove down the narrow road, Nancy saw an old black saloon parked along one side.

The dusty leaves of some sprawling bushes lay across the top of the car and hung down over the windscreen and other windows. It was impossible to see inside.

"That's really an old-timer," Nancy thought, and wondered if anyone were inside it.

After she had passed the car, her eyes shifted to the rear-view mirror. Slowing up, she studied the licence number plate, which was so mud-splattered that only four digits showed: 2-21-1.

Nancy's interest quickened at once. These were the first four numbers on the pigeon's leg band! Was there a connection?

She gave the licence number plate another fleeting glance and noted by the colour that it was from another state, but she could not see the identifying initials.

A moment later an oncoming car passed her. The driver raised a hand and called, "Hello, Nancy!"

"Dr Spire!" she exclaimed.

The famous bone specialist, a friend of the Drew family, was often called out on local emergencies. Glancing back again, Nancy was surprised to see Dr Spire pull up behind the old saloon.

Wondering if she could be of help, Nancy stopped at the side of the road and watched as the physician walked towards the parked car carrying his black bag. As he reached the saloon, a rear door swung open. Dr Spire put one foot inside and leaned forward. With a sudden movement he vanished into the car and it roared away.

"That was strange!" Nancy said aloud. "It seemed as if someone jerked him into the back seat. He may have been kidnapped!"

On a hunch, Nancy backed her convertible to the physician's car, then braked and leaped out. Dr Spire had locked his car and the keys were gone.

"I guess he expected to be met," Nancy told herself. "He probably jumped into the old saloon. But the whole thing is peculiar."

When Nancy reached home, Mrs Gruen opened the front door "It's here. Came a few minutes ago." She handed over a telegram.

Nancy tore open the envelope. The telegram was from the Pigeon Fanciers association. It read:

LOCAL REPRESENTATIVE WILL CALL. BIRD NOT REGISTERED. SUSPECT TROUBLE. KEEP MESSAGE SECRET

· 2 ·

A Golden Clue

"ANOTHER strange message!" remarked Hannah Gruen. "What do you think now, Nancy?"

"That a real mystery has dropped into my lap." Nancy grinned. "And about time! I've been longing for one. I can't wait to tell Dad about this!"

Carson Drew had always been close to his daughter, and often discussed his cases with her, because she grasped the issues so clearly and quickly.

Nancy re-read the telegram and said to Mrs Gruen, "The pigeon isn't registered. That's so its messages can't be traced to the sender."

Hannah replied, "Well, it takes all kinds of folks to make a world. What's more, pigeons, planes and telegrams aren't getting tonight's dinner ready. We're having a chicken casserole, one of your father's favourites."

"And mine," said Nancy.

"Mr Drew likes sweet pickles too," Hannah added. "I'll go down to the cellar and get a jar."

Nancy's thoughts returned to the odd message which had been attached to the pigeon's leg. She took the note from her pocket and studied it again. The words were neatly printed in black ink.

For safe-keeping, Nancy slipped the note and the

telegram into her handbag, and set it on the hall table. At that moment she heard a thumping noise and a cry from the cellar.

"Hannah!" she called. There was no answer.

Nancy dashed to the kitchen and looked down the cellar stairs. A huddled figure lay on the floor.

"Oh!" Nancy exclaimed and ran down the steps.

The housekeeper managed to sit up. "I slipped," she said shakily. "Oh, my back!"

"Hannah!" Nancy exclaimed anxiously. "Are you badly hurt?"

"No," the housekeeper replied. "I can get up, I'm sure. Just give me a hand."

Nancy put one arm round Hannah and helped the woman to her feet. Mrs Gruen stood still a few moments to catch her breath, then said:

"I guess I didn't break anything, thank goodness. But I'm afraid I've strained my back."

"I'll drive you to Dr Spire's," Nancy said, "and let him examine you." With the girl's help, the housekeeper slowly climbed the stairs.

"I have to get dinner," Hannah announced.

"That can wait," Nancy said firmly. "We'll leave a note telling Dad where we've gone."

As they drove towards the doctor's residence and office, Nancy hoped that he was back from his mysterious call. When they reached the house, Mrs Spire told them her husband was out.

"Is he still on that case out near the Blenheim estate?" Nancy asked. "I passed him on my way home from the flower show."

"Yes, he is, but he should be home soon." She and Nancy helped Hannah to a couch in the office. Then

Mrs Spire excused herself to get dinner, and asked Nancy to answer the office phone if it should ring. Twenty minutes later it buzzed.

Nancy lifted the receiver, but before she could say "Hello", a muffled voice asked if Dr Spire had returned. When Nancy said No, the caller directed her to write down a message.

As she wrote, a strange expression crossed her face. At the end of the message, the speaker abruptly hung up.

"Can I believe my eyes?" Nancy wondered as she looked at the message she had jotted down.

"If you say blue bells, you will get into trouble, for they are no longer used here."

"Blue bells again!" Nancy told herself. Was Dr Spire somehow involved in the mystery of the message attached to the pigeon's leg? Could it be more than coincidence that the numbers on the licence number plate of the black saloon matched the first four digits on the bird's leg band? Her suspicion that the doctor had been pulled forcibly into the saloon came flooding back.

Nancy was about to tell Hannah what the anonymous caller had said, when brisk footsteps were heard outside the door. Dr Spire, a lanky, balding man, strode into the office. Although he looked worried, his thin, intense face lighted with a smile.

"Well, Nancy, we meet again!"

Hiding her surprise and relief at seeing him safe, Nancy replied with a cheerful greeting.

The physician turned to Hannah. "Mrs Gruen, my wife has told me of your accident. I'm sorry to hear about it. I'll take a look at you now."

Fifteen minutes later the doctor announced that she had a strained back. "Rest in bed a few days. I'll write a prescription for you. In ten days you'll be feeling like your old self."

"I'll see that she rests," Nancy promised.

She helped Hannah to the car and settled her comfortably in the front seat. Then she excused herself and hurried back inside. The doctor was seated at his desk, gazing into space. He looked at Nancy inquiringly.

"I jotted down this phone message for you," she said. "It is important that I ask you something about it."

The doctor's lips tightened as he read the message. "Does it make sense to you?" Nancy asked.

"Yes," he said grimly.

Dr Spire stood up and strode across the room. Then he turned and faced Nancy. "I need help in solving a strange mystery. There's nobody with whom I'd rather discuss it than you and your father. Will you help me?"

"Of course," Nancy replied.

"Then will you both come back later?"

Nancy agreed. "I'm eager to hear your story. I think the mystery may be linked to one I'm working on."

The doctor looked amazed, but before he could ask what she meant, Mrs Spire came to tell him that dinner was ready. Nancy quickly excused herself.

When she and Hannah reached home, Carson Drew, a tall, distinguished-looking man, was eagerly waiting for them. He was sorry to hear what had happened to the housekeeper and helped her upstairs. After Mrs Gruen was settled in bed, Nancy brought her a tray of food, then prepared dinner for her father and herself.

While they ate, Nancy told him about the strange

occurrences. Mr Drew shook his head and chuckled. "You attract mystery like nectar in a flower attracts a bee, Nancy."

She grinned. "In this case, I'll be the blossom and hope the villain will come my way!"

"I'll go with you tonight," he agreed, "and I'll do anything I can to help."

With a twinkle in her eyes Nancy said, "Then you can start clearing the table. I'll scrape the dishes and put them in the dish-washer."

Carson Drew laughed. "You caught me that time, young lady!"

But he was Nancy's willing helper and it did not take the father-daughter team long to tidy the kitchen. Then they set off for Dr Spire's office. He greeted them cordially and indicated deep leather armchairs.

Mr Drew said quietly, "Suppose you tell us what's worrying you, Richard."

"It's a strange story," the physician said. "I almost can't believe it myself. This afternoon I had a phone call saying that a patient of mine, Mrs Manning Smith, had been in a minor car accident on Hollow Hill Road. She wanted me to meet her there and if necessary take her to the hospital.

"The caller—a man—told me to look for an old black saloon. Since I know Mrs Smith has such a car, I thought nothing of it. After passing you on the road, Nancy, I spotted the car, parked, and went up to it. The back door swung open. As I leaned forward to look inside, my shoulders were seized and I was yanked to the floor. Before I could move, a hood was dropped over my head and a man on each side held me firmly."

"How far did you travel?" Nancy asked.

"A long time—about an hour. Not a word was spoken during the trip."

"Where did they take you?" Mr Drew asked.

"I don't know. But some of the roads were bumpy. I think we were out in the country. When the hood was finally removed I found myself in what appeared to be a hospital room."

"Was there a patient?" Nancy asked eagerly.

"Yes, but not Mrs Smith. Someone explained a clerk had made a mistake. I didn't learn the patient's name. She was an elderly woman, suffering from a dislocated shoulder. There was just one other person in the room—a nurse. She was a large, hard-faced woman and warned me not to talk to the patient."

"Did you try?" Mr Drew queried.

"No, but all the time I was working, it seemed as if she wanted to tell me something. Her eyes kept flashing signals which I could not understand. Then, while I was taking her pulse, the nurse turned for a moment and the woman slipped this into my hand."

Dr Spire reached into his pocket and held out a thin, gold-chain bracelet with a small gold shield dangling from it.

"How dainty!" Nancy exclaimed as she took the bracelet to examine it. Set into the bangle was a garnet.

"There's an inscription over the jewel," she said. " 'To my darling Mary from Joe.' " Nancy turned the shield over. "On the other side is a coat of arms. Perhaps we could trace it and find out the woman's name. If she's being held against her will, we ought to rescue her!"

"It's worth a try," her father agreed.

"Keep the bracelet, Nancy," the doctor said, "and see what you can learn about it." Then he continued his story. "When I finished, two men came in and replaced the hood. Then I was driven back to my car. A couple of times when I tried to resist, they got rough."

"How dreadful!" Nancy burst out. "Dr Spire, do you think the woman was able to talk, but had been ordered not to?"

"Yes, I do."

"Did you see or hear anything that would help us find the place?"

Dr Spire smiled. "I learned the password to the place."

"Marvellous!" said Nancy. "What was it?"

He replied, "As we turned into a driveway—I could tell by the creak of gates—the driver said 'Bluebells' and someone answered 'Pass'."

Nancy's eyes sparkled with excitement. "This is where my story comes in, Dr Spire." Quickly she told him about the pigeon, the plane, and the telegram. "Whoever is holding the woman prisoner must have been afraid you had heard the password. So he decided to change it."

"Yes, that would have been just about five o'clock, as the pigeon message said," the physician agreed. "The phone call here was to warn me not to try finding the place again or using the password to get in if I did."

Carson Drew spoke up. "Richard, you must report this to the police."

Just then the telephone rang. When the physician finished the call, he said, "Emergency at the hospital.

I'll have to go. Carson, will you and Nancy report the incident to the police for me?"

"We'll stop at headquarters," the lawyer replied.

As the Drews left the house, Nancy noticed a shadowy figure across the street. "Are we being watched?" the young sleuth wondered.

While driving into town Nancy noted a pair of headlights reflected in her mirror. One was dimmer than the other. The uneven lights stayed close behind all the way to police headquarters. Nancy slowed down in front of the building, and the car, a sleek black saloon, went past.

"No place to park here, Dad," she said. "Suppose you hop out and start telling your story. I'll join you as soon as I find a parking space."

Mr Drew got out, and a few minutes later Nancy pulled into the far side of a car park at the corner. When she stepped out of the car, a hulky figure emerged from the nearby shadows.

A feeling of apprehension swept over Nancy, and she tried to dart past the man. But a powerful hand seized her arm and jerked her back.

"Not so fast!" the stranger growled in a deep voice.

· 3 ·

A Chase

"LET me go or I'll scream!" Nancy cried out.

Instantly the man released her arm, but he swiftly stepped in front of her. "Wait a minute," he commanded. "You want to help your father, don't you?"

"I don't know what you're talking about," Nancy said warily. She studied the husky, broad-shouldered man. He had heavy brows, deep-set eyes, and a cruel mouth.

"You're Nancy Drew, aren't you?"

Nancy hesitated, afraid he might be trying to find her father to harm him. "Are you sure you're talking to the right person?" she asked.

"Okay," the man said bitterly, "play it smart. It's been years since I saw Drew, and maybe I'm wrong. But I could be right, so you take a message."

Nancy did not reply, and the stranger went on, "Tell Carson Drew to mind his own business or he's in for a bad shock."

"If you're through," Nancy said coldly, "I'll go now."

The man stepped aside and she hurried from the car park, her heart pounding. As she reached the pavement Nancy came face to face with two friends.

"Why, Nancy Drew!" exclaimed Jean Moss. "I

haven't seen you for weeks!" Her escort, Bill Wright, added, "Been solving any mysteries lately?"

Nancy's heart sank. Had the man in the car park heard them? She managed to talk pleasantly with the couple for a few minutes but she was worried.

As Jean and Bill moved off, Nancy heard a soft laugh from the shadows. A moment later a deep voice said mockingly, "Good night, Miss Drew." The speaker melted into the darkness.

Biting her lip in vexation, Nancy ran to police head-quarters. The officer on duty directed her to the Detective Bureau. Here Mr Drew was conferring with Lieutenant Mulligan, a red-faced, brawny man with thinning hair. He knew the Drews only by reputation.

Once again Nancy told her story. The detective jotted down the partial licence number of the suspicious car.

When Nancy handed him the bracelet, he said, "Hmm. Has an inscription, but it's old. Mary and Joe could have been dead for years. No last name or dates, either. Afraid it won't be much use to us."

"If you don't mind," Nancy said, "I'd like to see if I can trace the owner."

"Go ahead," the lieutenant said and gave it back. "We'll check out the car's licence number, but probably the kidnappers are using phoney plates."

As Nancy and her father walked back to the car park, she told him about the stranger who had accosted her there and the warning message.

Mr Drew frowned. "I don't know who he could be. Some crank, I suppose."

Cars were closely parked on either side of Nancy's convertible, so she gave her full attention to pulling out of the tight space. Soon after she had driven into the street and turned towards home, headlights appeared in her mirror. The right one was dim!

"Dad, the same car that followed us before is behind us," Nancy said tensely. "I'm afraid the driver's the man who wants to harm you! Let's try to shake him."

Keeping within the speed limit, Nancy drove into the residential section of the city, taking every short cut and winding street she knew. Meanwhile Mr Drew watched the car behind, which continued to follow.

"It seems useless to try getting away," he said finally. "I'd like to get a good look at the driver."

"All right," Nancy replied.

She increased her speed, widening the distance between the two cars, until she approached an intersection where there was a bright overhead light. She swung round, her tyres squealing on the asphalt, and stopped short, facing her pursuer.

When he came abreast of them, Carson Drew gasped. "Follow him!" the lawyer ordered as the driver zoomed off.

Nancy turned again and pursued the saloon. Just as she was about to overtake it, the traffic light ahead turned red. The driver rode straight through, rounded a corner, and disappeared.

Nancy sighed. "We'll never find him now."

"Never mind," said Mr Drew. "It was a good try. Let's go home."

"Who was that man, Dad?" Nancy asked.

"Adam Thorne, an escaped convict. Thank goodness, he didn't hurt you."

Nancy shuddered. "What was he jailed for?"

"Thorne was given ten years for embezzling the

assets of an estate. While in jail he became very bitter and at times violent."

"But what's his interest in you?" Nancy queried.

Mr Drew explained that Thorne had been a River Heights lawyer. "He was disbarred prior to his trial and I was in charge of gathering the evidence against him."

"I see," said Nancy. "Dad, I have a hunch Adam Thorne is involved in the bluebell mystery. He must have been spying outside Dr Spire's house and recognized you. Probably he's not only looking for revenge, but wants to keep us from working on the case."

"I'm afraid you're right. For Pete's sake be careful, Nancy."

"You too, Dad."

A few minutes later the Drews reached home. While Nancy checked on Hannah, who was asleep, Mr Drew called Lieutenant Mulligan and reported his daughter's encounter with Adam Thorne and the resultant, unsuccessful chase.

"If Thorne's tied in with Dr Spire's kidnapping," said Mulligan, "he'll stop at nothing. I'll broadcast a bulletin immediately."

The next morning Nancy was up early and went to talk to Hannah Gruen.

"I have good news for you," the housekeeper said. "My niece Effie has offered to come here and work while I'm laid up."

"Good. Effie's fun."

"And scatter-brained sometimes," Hannah remarked.

After breakfast Nancy drove off to get Effie Schneider. When she rang the bell of the small timber cottage, the door was opened by Effie's mother.

"Hello, Mrs Schneider," said Nancy. "How are you?"

"Fine thanks. Please come in. Effie isn't dressed yet. She's been reading a movie magazine instead of putting on her clothes . . . Effie!" she called.

"Here I am, Mum," a high-pitched voice replied. "Hi, Nancy!" said the girl as she walked into the living-room munching a banana.

"Hello, Effie," Nancy greeted the thin, seventeen-year-old girl.

Effie had light-blonde hair, which she wore close-cropped with a feathery fringe over her forehead. She was dressed in a Chinese-style pink kimono, with high-heeled satin mules.

"This outfit is like the one Ling Su wore in the movie, 'The Chinese Wall Mystery'," Effie remarked, making an Oriental bow.

Nancy grinned, but Mrs Schneider said tartly, "Hurry up and put on street clothes, Effie." As her daughter went off, Mrs Schneider turned to Nancy. "Once Effie stops mooning about movie stars and singers, she's really a good worker and a fine cook."

Nancy had her doubts about this, but later was agreeably surprised when Effie prepared a delicious luncheon of chicken salad, hot rolls, and iced tea. She would not let Nancy help her.

"Aunt Hannah told me you're working on a mystery," Effie said. "That's exciting. You keep your mind on the case. I'll do the work around the house. I once read a mystery about a circus girl who was shot out of a cannon and disappeared. It took three detectives a whole month to find her. Bet you can't guess where."

Nancy grinned. "Inside the cannon?"

"Oh gee, how'd you know? Effie said. "You must have read the story.

"No, I didn't."

Bewildered, Effie shook her head and walked off. After eating lunch, Nancy decided to start tracing the owner of the bracelet. Half an hour later she walked into Butler and Stone's jewellery shop and asked for Mr Stone, who was a personal friend.

"Well, Nancy, what can I do for you?" the jeweller asked cordially. "Are you interested in a diamond-studded detective badge today?" he teased.

Nancy laughed. "Do you sell them?" she countered.

"Oh sure. To the police," the jeweller replied with a grin.

Nancy took the bracelet from her purse. "Mr Stone, could you trace this coat of arms?"

The jeweller held the bracelet towards the window to get a better look at the heraldic design on the shield. As he did so, Nancy noticed a large woman in a pink butterfly-print dress looking through the plate-glass window.

"Just a moment," Nancy said quickly to Mr Stone. "Is there some other place—"

The jeweller understood at once. "Another mystery?" he asked.

When Nancy nodded, he motioned to a private office at the back of the shop. Once again Mr Stone examined the bracelet. "This was made in Victorian times," he announced. "I doubt if it was designed round here. Hmm, an attractive coat of arms. Three mullets dexter and a Maltese cross sinister; crest, a falcon's head embattled, with the motto 'Esse quam videre'.

"Every authentic coat of arms is a matter of record," Mr Stone explained. "It will take time, but we will be able to trace the family, if not the individual owner. May I keep the bracelet temporarily?"

Nancy hesitated. "It doesn't belong to me," she said. "Could you make a copy of the crest?"

"Certainly. Please take a seat." Mr Stone excused himself and went out. In fifteen minutes he returned, gave the bracelet to Nancy, and said he would send the tracing to a Mr Abelard de Gotha, an expert on coats of arms.

"Thank you. I'll stop by in a couple of days to see if you've heard about it," Nancy said.

As the young detective left the store her thoughts turned to the sick woman who had given the bracelet to Dr Spire.

"I wonder who she is, poor thing."

At the corner Nancy waited with a group of people for the light to change. As the walk signal came on, someone pushed roughly past her and darted out into the street. Nancy recognized the pink butterfly-print dress and at the same moment realized that her arm felt strangely light.

"My handbag!" Nancy gasped. "It's gone!"

The woman was hurrying ahead of the crowd. Nancy was sure she had stolen the bag and sprinted after her.

"Stop!" Nancy shouted, but the woman broke into a run.

Nancy put on a spurt of speed and caught up with her on the far pavement. "Give me back my—"

The big woman whirled and gave Nancy a powerful push that sent her reeling. She fell backwards off the pavement!

· 4 ·

Frightened Grandparents

SEVERAL quick-acting pedestrians caught Nancy just before she hit the road.

"Are you hurt?" exclaimed a middle-aged woman as she helped the girl to her feet. "I saw that awful woman push you. Were you trying to catch her?"

Nancy took a deep breath and said, "Yes. She has stolen my handbag," then added, "I'm all right. Thanks so much."

Suddenly Nancy spotted the thief hurrying into Brent's Department Store down the street. She dashed after her and hastened through the revolving doors.

Looking round quickly, Nancy saw a flash of pink near the lifts. By the time she reached them, the woman had gone up in one of the lifts.

Nancy darted to the nearby escalator and rushed up, two steps at a time. On the second floor she sped to the lifts but saw by the indicator light that the one she wanted had already left. The woman was not in sight.

"What luck!" Nancy murmured, darting back to the escalator.

A few moments later she arrived breathless on the third floor. As Nancy looked towards the lift, the door was starting to close. No one was inside. The woman she was after must have stepped off here!

"May I help you?" asked a salesgirl. "We have some lovely—"

"No, no!" Nancy panted. "I'm after a thief! A woman in a pink print dress. Did you see her get off the elevator?"

The girl's eyes grew wide. "A thief!" she exclaimed. "Why, yes, I did see her, but I don't know where she went. What did she take?"

"My handbag," said Nancy.

"I'll get my supervisor," said the salesgirl.

Nancy glanced round the third floor, where many customers were examining racks of dresses. Where could the woman be hiding?

"Dressing-rooms," Nancy decided. She saw that the Autumn Clothes Department had fewer customers than the others. "I'll start there."

She hastened across the floor and peered through an archway into a narrow aisle. There was a row of curtained cubicles along one wall.

Quietly Nancy peeked into the first room. Empty! In the next a stout woman was struggling into a tight dress. She did not see Nancy. Quickly the young detective moved along the row of dressing-rooms. In the fifth room she found the thief!

The woman was leaning against the wall, panting. Nancy's open handbag lay on a shelf beside her and in one hand the woman clutched the gold-chain bracelet.

"I'll take that!" Nancy said, stepping into the cubicle.

The woman froze in amazement for a moment, then swiftly seized the handbag and hurled it at Nancy. As the girl ducked, the contents scattered and the woman tried to dash past. Nancy seized her wrist and caught hold of the bracelet.

"Help! Thief!" she shouted.

Instantly the woman let go of the gold chain, broke free, and raced into the corridor, with Nancy at her heels. The thief darted through the arch, but as Nancy reached it, two saleswomen arrived, blocking the way.

"What happened?" one asked.

"That woman in pink!" Nancy exclaimed. "I must stop her!" She darted round the salesladies and ran towards the lifts.

Too late! She saw the thief board a lift just before the door closed.

How to stop her? Suddenly Nancy spotted a store telephone behind a nearby counter. She hurried to it and picked up the receiver.

"Operator, this is an emergency! Ring the phone nearest the entrance on Main Street, please!"

In a second a voice said, "Silverware!"

"Listen carefully," Nancy said tersely. "A large woman in a pink print dress will probably come rushing towards you any minute now, heading for the door. Stop her! She's a thief!"

"Just a moment," said the girl. There was a pause, then the speaker said, "The woman you described passed my counter as we were talking. I ran after her, but she hopped into a taxi and it sped off. Shall I notify the store detective?"

"No, thanks," said Nancy. "It's too late."

Disappointed, she hung up, as a voice behind her said, "What's going on?"

Nancy turned round. It was Mr Mahoney, the store manager. He was surrounded by salesladies. One gave

Nancy her handbag with all the contents restored.

"Oh, hello, Nancy," said Mr Mahoney. "What's this about a thief in the store?"

Nancy took him aside and explained briefly. "I don't think the woman is an ordinary bag snatcher. She's probably mixed up in a case I'm working on."

"Well, I hope you catch her," Mr Mahoney said. He waved goodbye and walked off.

Nancy examined her handbag. The strap had been cut. "I doubt if that woman knew I had the bracelet with me before she saw it through the jeweller's window." The young detective suspected that Adam Thorne had engaged the thief to follow her.

"I believe she recognized the bracelet," Nancy told herself, "and she'll tell Thorne about it. I hope the old lady who owns it doesn't get into trouble for slipping it to Dr Spire."

Nancy was deep in thought as she walked down the street, and did not see a petite, dark-haired young woman hurrying towards her.

"Nancy! What luck to run into you!"

"Helen Corning! Oh, I'm sorry," Nancy said with a grin. "I can't get used to your being Mrs Archer. How's everything?"

"Oh, just great, except for one thing. Nancy, I was going to call you this very afternoon. How about solving a mystery for me?"

Seeing her friend's look of interest, she chuckled. "I thought that would catch you. Could you come to my apartment tomorrow evening at six? I'll tell you all about it then. Besides, Jim would love to see you."

"I wouldn't miss it," Nancy replied, "but I think it's only fair to tell you I'm already working on a mystery."

Helen smiled. "Then this is just one more. You're so clever, Nancy, I'm sure you can solve both at once!"

Nancy laughed. "Give me a hint."

Helen explained that her Grandmother and Grandfather Corning had recently moved to Sylvan Lake. "They have a dreamy stone house on a hill. It is beautiful. But now Gram and Gramp are afraid to stay there because of something queer that keeps happening."

"What is it?" Nancy asked.

Helen glanced at her watch. "I'd love to tell you, but I must run. See you tomorrow. We'll drive out to the lake and have dinner with Gram and Gramp. Thanks a million, Nancy!"

As Helen Archer hurried away, Nancy stood on the pavement musing. "Um—another case." Then she turned towards home.

When Nancy reached it, Effie opened the front door. "I heard you coming," she said in a loud whisper. "The pigeon man's here." She gestured towards the living-room. "He's very good-looking."

"Thank you," said Nancy, and went to greet the caller, hoping he had not heard Effie.

A tall blond man in his twenties got up as she entered. He introduced himseld as Donald Jordan, secretary of the local branch of the Pigeon Fanciers association. He showed her his credentials.

"I'm so glad you came," said Nancy. "Please sit down. I'll get the pigeon and the message."

Nancy hurried to the garage and saw with relief that the bird seemed stronger.

"Oh, I hope Mr Jordan won't take you away," she murmured to the bird. "I want you to get well enough to fly to your home loft. Then I'll follow you!"

Nancy carried the pigeon to the living-room. Mr Jordan examined the bird gently, noting especially the number on its leg band. Then Nancy took the message from her bag and handed it to him.

"This is the second pigeon seen in this area with an unregistered number," he said. "The other was found dead on the highway. I mentioned it to a detective friend of mine. He thought criminals might be using this means of communication, thinking it safer than telephone or telegraph or letter."

Nancy nodded and told him she had reported the incident to the police.

"Good. That saves us the trouble." The young man arose. "Well, thank you for notifying me, Miss Drew. Now I'll take the bird and—"

"Oh, please don't!" Nancy exclaimed.

Mr Jordan looked surprised. "Surely you don't want to be bothered with a sick pigeon?"

"I don't mind," said Nancy. "I'd like to try to nurse it back to health."

The young man shook his head. "I'm afraid there's not much chance, but if that's what you want, it's okay with me."

He made copies of the leg-band number and the strange message, then wished her luck and left. Nancy returned the pigeon to the garage. She immediately went to Hannah Gruen's room to tell her about the latest developments in the case.

"And about time," said the housekeeper. "I never hear any news up here."

"How are you feeling?" Nancy asked.

"Much better. If it wasn't for that fussy doctor, I'd be up and working like I should."

Nancy laughed. "You just take it easy while you have the chance!"

Late in the afternoon Mr Drew called to say that he could not be home until eight o'clock. To keep Hannah company, Nancy and Effie ate dinner on trays in her room and afterwards watched a television play.

At the end, Effie sniffed in disappointment. "Not enough love," she commented. "Now that handsome Mr Kyle should have—"

She stopped speaking as the front doorbell rang. "Dad must have forgotten his key," Nancy remarked. "I'll go."

She hurried down the stairs and started to open the door. Instinct told the young sleuth to be cautious. She flicked the wall switch to turn on the porch light, then opened the door a crack. The porch was dark! Nancy thought the bulb must have burned out.

"Dad?" Nancy called quickly.

There was no answer, but from somewhere in the shadows came the sound of heavy breathing.

· 5 ·

Blue Fire

"Who's there?" Nancy called sharply into the darkness. She heard a stirring near the porch, but could see no one.

"Never mind who," came a rasping whisper from the shadows. "We warned your father to mind his own business. Now we're telling you: forget the doctor's story or you'll be sorry."

Just then headlights swept up the driveway. Instantly a dark figure dashed across the lawn and disappeared into the night.

Nancy recognized her father's car. Moments later Mr Drew parked beside the house and hurried up the porch steps.

"Is something wrong?" he asked. "Why are you out here?"

"A man rang the bell, Dad, but wouldn't let me see him. He gave us another warning."

The lawyer's face was grim. "Did you recognize his voice?" he asked.

"It sounded something like Adam Thorne's," Nancy replied, "but I can't be sure because he spoke in a whisper. The man was big, though, like Thorne."

Nancy explained why the light was not on, and turned to examine it. "The bulb's gone!" she exclaimed. "I suppose the man took it out so I couldn't see him. I'll put in a new one."

"I'd like to wring that fellow's neck," her father stormed. "I'll put the car away, then report this to Lieutenant Mulligan."

"Dad, before you put the car in the garage, would you drive me to the flower show? I'm just a little bit curious as to who won the prizes."

He grinned. "Of course I'll take you." He patted her shoulder. "While I phone Mulligan, go tell Hannah and Effie where we're going and *not* to answer the doorbell."

Twenty minutes later father and daughter arrived at the greenhouse on the Blenheim estate. The display was beautiful, but the cut flowers were beginning to wilt. Nancy's pulse quickened as she approached her own entry.

"Dad!" she cried out. "Look!"

Attached to her bouquet of larkspur was a dark-blue satin ribbon with the inscription FIRST PRIZE!

"Nancy, that's wonderful," her father said. "Congratulations! Maybe you ought to give up solving mysteries and raise flowers."

"Not a chance," she said.

"But it's far less dangerous," he countered. "Take this present mystery, for instance. It might be wise for you to drop it."

Nancy looked shocked. "Why, Dad! Think of the poor old woman who is a prisoner. '

"But, Nancy, my first concern is for your safety. You are more important to me than all the mysterious old ladies in the world!"

Nancy's face showed her disappointment. "Oh please, Dad, no."

With a crash Nancy's flowers were knocked to the ground

Mr Drew looked uncomfortable. "I know, I know. You're like me. You'll never be satisfied until you lick the problem. Go ahead."

"Thank you, Dad," Nancy said happily. "I will."

"Hold it, Miss Drew!" said a voice nearby.

Nancy looked up to see a news photographer pointing a camera at her. "There! Stand right next to your exhibit."

Before she could comply, Nancy heard another voice say, "Go get her!" At the same instant a big, vicious-looking dog sprang at her!

"Oh!" she screamed, dodging just in time. The Great Dane crashed into the vase of prize flowers, knocking the exhibit to the ground and shattering the vase. He yelped in fright, then ran off.

"Who owns that beast?" cried the photographer.

No one claimed to be the owner. The Drews guessed Thorne was behind the attack, but could see him nowhere in the crowd. He—or his henchmen—had taken advantage of the excitement to escape.

Nancy reported the incident to Mrs Winsor, who told her to take the blue ribbon home. When she and her father reached the house, Hannah and Effie were delighted to hear that Nancy had won first prize in the delphinium class. "Here's hoping," said Mrs Gruen, "that you'll come out ahead in your mystery, too."

"You're sweet," Nancy told the housekeeper, then kissed her good night without |telling of the dog episode. But she was alarmed over it.

Nancy went to her pretty yellow-and-white bedroom. There she changed into nightdress, dressing-gown and slippers, then seated herself at her desk. She was determined to figure out the strange message which the pigeon had been carrying.

She opened a gardening book and turned to blue-bells, then delphinium and larkspur. She learned that bluebells were different from the others. Delphinium was a perennial flower and usually blue, though some were white or lavender. Larkspur, the annual flower of the genus, occurred in pale and dark blue, mauve and other shades. In common usage, however, the names delphinium and larkspur were often inter-changed.

"Well, that's interesting," Nancy thought, "but it doesn't get me much further." She closed the book with a sigh and put it away. "Maybe if I just forget the whole thing until morning an answer will come to me."

She stretched out on her comfortable bed and tuned in the clock-radio to her favourite musical programme. But her mind kept returning to the problem.

"I have larkspur on the brain. Larkspur—larkspur," she mused, clasping her hands behind her head. "Funny name. I wonder how they came to be called that. Maybe because the blossoms have little points or spurs. But why the lark? Why not sparrowspur or ostrichspur?

"Spurs are for horses, and horses don't look like larks, and larks don't suggest anything that wear spurs. Larks sing and—Oh!" Nancy sat bolt upright. "I have it! I'll bet that's it!"

She raced to her father's study and knocked. Mr Drew called, "Come in." He looked up from the letter he was writing when Nancy exclaimed:

"Dad! I think I have a clue to the kidnappers' hide-out. It's larkspur! *Singing horses* stands for lark—spurs!"

"Nancy, that could be it!"

"Maybe the kidnappers got the idea of using that flower in their code, because it grows at the headquarters of the gang!"

The lawyer nodded thoughtfully as Nancy went on, "There may be bluebells there too, but I'm not sure. *Blue bells* in the pigeon's message might mean something else since it is two words. I'm going to drive through the countryside until I find a place—a house, a street, or something else—that has larkspurs, bluebells, or both as its most conspicuous feature."

"It's certainly a lead worth working on," said her father. "Better than trying to follow the pigeon to its home loft."

In the morning Nancy studied a map of the River Heights area and decided to ride through the countryside east of the town on her search for the tell-tale flowers. She drove tirelessly, stopping only to ask people if they could direct her to places where either larkspurs or bluebells grew. Here and there she found larkspurs in gardens of private homes too small to be the place Dr Spire had described. After lunch she drove on, but had no luck. At four o'clock she gave up, disappointed.

"My score is exactly zero," she thought. "Well, tonight I hear about the Corning mystery."

Back home again, Nancy went to Hannah Gruen's room to see how the housekeeper was getting along. "I'm feeling much better," Hannah reported, and told Nancy that her father would not be home for supper.

Nancy showered, put on a pretty lime-green dress with a matching sweater, and left the house. Twenty minutes later she was ringing the bell of Helen's apartment flat. The door was opened by Helen's handsome husband, Jim Archer.

"Hi, Nancy!" he said, smiling. "We're ready."

"Jim will drive his car out to the lake," Helen said as she came into the living-room. "Leave yours here."

On the way, Helen asked about Nancy's two close girl friends, Bess Marvin and her cousin George Fayne. "How are they?"

"They've been holidaying in California," said Nancy, "but they're coming home tomorrow." She chuckled. "Won't they be surprised when I tell them I have two mysteries they can help me solve!"

Helen grinned. "It's my guess they won't be a bit surprised!"

Presently Jim turned on to the side road which led to the lake. When they reached it, the setting sun had turned the water to a golden colour. A few sail-boats, silhouetted against the red sky, were heading towards shore.

"What a lovely scene!" Nancy exclaimed.

The road circled the lake and at one point branched on to a drive which led up the wooded hillside. The Corning's modern house was nestled among the trees and rocks at the top, overlooking the water. The drive wound around it to a large flagstoned area, surrounded by shrubs. Jim parked the car there.

"The front door is at the back," Helen said with a laugh as she led the way to it and rang the bell.

The door was opened by a middle-aged man-servant with red hair. He wore neat dark trousers and a white jacket.

"Hello, Morgan," Helen said cheerfully. "How are you?"

"All right, thank you," he answered, but did not

smile. Nancy wondered if he, too, was worried about the strange happenings here.

Mrs Corning hurried into the hall to greet her guests. She was a pretty woman, with short fluffy white hair, and just as petite as Helen. She took them into the big living-room with a huge picture window.

Mr Corning rose from a chair. He was a tall man with a bold, aristocratic nose. Though he had to use a cane to support his frail-looking body, his dark eyes were alert and usually sparkled with humour. But now, Nancy noted, there was a strained expression on his face.

"What is frightening the Cornings?" Nancy wondered.

She had no hint until after dinner when the group returned to the living-room. As the girls seated themselves in deep pumpkin-coloured chairs, Mrs Corning went to the window. She began to draw the soft beige curtains, shutting out the dark wooded hillside below and the few lights of houses on the opposite shore.

"Oh, please leave the curtains open, Gram," said Helen. "Let's watch for the thing tonight. After all, that's what Nancy's here for."

"Thing?" Nancy repeated, leaning forward in her chair. "Please tell me about it."

"Of course," said Mr Corning. As his wife opened the curtains again, he began, "One night about two weeks ago, my wife and I were sitting here enjoying the view when we saw a large circle of blue fire at the bottom of the hill."

"Blue fire!" Nancy exclaimed.

Mr Corning nodded. "Yes, it's a circle about as big as a car wheel, and glows with an eerie blue fire. It's approximately seven feet off the ground."

"Sounds weird," Helen remarked.

"How long did it last?" Nancy asked.

"About five minutes—then vanished. The next night it came again—this time closer."

"We've seen the thing every night since," put in Mrs Corning. "It has come nearer each time. Somehow, I feel it is a threat."

"In the meantime," her husband went on, "there have been strange happenings in the house. I want to show you something." He arose unsteadily, then suddenly gasped. Seizing the chair back with one hand, he pointed with his cane out of the huge window.

"There's that spooky blue flame again!"

Nancy leaped to her feet. In the darkness of the woods, not far below the house, glowed a large blue fiery circle.

"Helen! Jim!" Nancy exclaimed. "Let's go see what it is!"

"Be careful!" Mrs Corning urged as the young people dashed from the room. The trio let themselves out of the main door.

"Helen and I will go to the right," Nancy whispered. "Jim, you take the left. When we're even with the light, let's close in on it."

As Jim slipped away in the darkness, the girls went quietly down through the woods. The blue circle continued to burn steadily.

"Queer," Nancy murmured. "What is it?"

Unfortunately, Helen slipped on a stone and turned her ankle. Involuntarily she gave a cry of pain. Both girls froze, their hearts pounding.

For a moment the circle of light did not move. Then, slowly, it began to turn towards them!

· 6 ·

Mysterious Morgan

HELEN seized Nancy's arm as the eerie blue circle of fire moved towards them through the woods. Nancy squeezed her friend's hand reassuringly, though she herself was not certain that the ring meant harm to them.

Closer and closer it came. Suddenly Helen could stand the suspense no longer and gave a shrill scream. *Instantly the circle vanished!*

Nancy darted to the place it had been, but now nothing was there. She tried to peer through the darkness, but the night seemed blacker than ever.

At the same time, she could hear Jim shouting for Helen and running towards them. "What's the matter?" he panted.

"That weird fire was coming at us," said Helen. "I lost my head and screamed. I'm sorry, Nancy," she added. "It spoiled your chance to find out what the thing was."

"Never mind. I'll see it again, I'm sure."

Back in the house, the Cornings met the three with a flood of anxious questions. They had heard Helen scream and were badly shaken. Quietly Nancy explained what had happened.

"I'll ring for Morgan," said Helen's grandmother.

"I think we could all do with a cup of tea to settle our nerves." She pushed a button on the low table beside her.

Five minutes later the manservant had not yet appeared. "I'll go for him, Gram," Jim offered, but returned to report that he could not find him. "I looked everywhere, including his room."

"Perhaps he went outside to investigate the blue fire," Nancy suggested. "I think we ought to search the woods for him."

"I went out and called," said Jim, "but got no answer."

The elder Cornings exchanged worried glances. "Never mind, Gram," said Helen. "I'll make the tea. You tell Nancy the rest of the story."

"It was two weeks ago," said Mrs Corning, "that we first saw the circle of fire. And it was exactly two weeks ago that Morgan changed."

"How do you mean?" Nancy asked.

"He used to be such a cheerful fellow," she replied, "always ready with a little joke. Nothing we asked was ever too much trouble. I can't tell you what a tower of strength he has been. Over the years he has become like a member of the family. But now—he's a stranger."

"He forgets things," said Mr Corning. "Sometimes we ring and he doesn't come. Afterwards he mumbles a flimsy excuse."

"Several times I heard noises at night on the ground floor," said Mrs Corning. "I came down and found Morgan wandering around, fully dressed, with a strange, frightened look on his face. We've asked him a number of times to tell us what's the matter, but he avoids answering."

"How long have you known him?" Nancy asked.

"Fifteen years," replied her host. "He came to us with excellent references. And now I don't know what we would do without him."

"Perhaps he needs medical help," Nancy suggested.

"Maybe he does," said Mrs Corning, "but I feel sure the reason for his trouble is the blue fire." She arose, went to a modern-looking desk, and returned with an envelope. From it she took a folded card.

"On the morning of the day the fire first appeared," said Mrs Corning, "a letter came in the post for Morgan. A little later when I went to the kitchen, he was sitting in a chair, very pale, with his hand on his heart. The open envelope was on the table but the card had dropped to the floor. As I picked it up, I couldn't help noticing it was an ordinary greeting card."

"Did you see a signature?" Nancy asked. Helen's grandmother shook her head.

Mrs Corning explained that they had called a doctor, who said Morgan had suffered a bad shock. But the manservant would answer no questions.

"That afternoon," Mrs Corning went on, "I called a taxi and went to the little shopping centre across the lake. I found a duplicate of the card there. I wanted to get a close look at it." She handed the card to Nancy.

On the front of the card was the picture of an attractive cottage with the door wide open. Above it were the words "OPEN THE WAY TO FRIENDSHIP". The inside was blank.

"Did you see any marks on the original?"

"None. It was exactly like this one—just an innocent card."

"Not so innocent, I'm afraid," said Nancy. "It had no signature and that makes me think the card was a message from someone Morgan knows and probably fears. Have you reported any of these happenings to the police?"

Mr Corning sighed. "We discussed doing so, but Morgan begged us not to. I thought he might have another attack if we did. No, Nancy, we'd like to get to the bottom of the matter quietly."

Helen returned with the tea trolley. As Mrs Corning poured, she suggested that the young people stay overnight. "To tell the truth, we'd feel better with you here."

They agreed and Nancy went to call her father. Before retiring, she asked, "Have any of the lake residents seen the blue fire?"

"There is only one other house near ours," Mr Corning replied, "but it's empty. Folks across the lake don't bother about what goes on here."

Jim spoke up. "Gram said Morgan often disappears for a while after the blue fire is seen. He probably spots it from his room, which is at the end of the house and faces the lake."

"I imagine he's back by now," said Mrs Corning. "I'll check after I show you to your rooms."

She led the three guests into the hall and up a spiral staircase. Nancy was given a room which had a full view of the lake.

"There are several nightdresses in the dresser," Mrs Corning told her. "Help yourself."

Nancy waited until her hostess had checked on Morgan. He had not returned! As the young sleuth got ready for bed, she wondered where the mysterious manservant had gone.

In the morning, when she followed Helen and Jim to the dining-room, Nancy found Mrs Corning setting the table while her husband watched, white-faced, from a chair.

Morgan was still missing!

"His bed hasn't been slept in," said Helen's grandmother, "and our car hasn't been used."

"He might be lying hurt in the woods," Nancy suggested. "We'd better search."

The three young people hurried towards the front door. But as Jim made to open it, Nancy exclaimed, "Wait!"

Sticking out from under the door was a piece of white paper. She picked up the paper and unfolded it. It contained a message written in pencil. Nancy read it aloud:

" 'Don't worry about me. Have to be away for a while. Don't call police. Will explain later.' " It was signed "Morgan".

"He must have slipped this under the door late last night," said Nancy.

The three returned to the dining-room and Nancy showed the note to Mrs Corning. "Yes," she said, "that is Morgan's handwriting."

"Gramp, I think you should call the police," said Helen.

Her grandfather shook his head. "For the present, we'll do as Morgan asks."

"Of course, we can get along without him for a day or two," said Mrs Corning, "but I'd feel safer if someone were here at night."

"I wish I could be here," said Helen, "but—"

"No, no," her grandmother said firmly. "Your place is with your husband."

"Perhaps Nancy could stay," Helen suggested. "Would you?" she asked her friend.

"I'd love to," said Nancy, "but you know I am also working on another case."

Mrs Corning smiled. "This could be your head-quarters for both." Suddenly she frowned. "But I don't like to think of you working on this case alone. It might be dangerous."

"Maybe Bess and George could come," Helen said eagerly. "You three could have lots of fun here when you're not working on your mysteries."

"I'll see what Dad says," Nancy promised. "Anyhow, I'll come back tonight. I'd like another chance to catch whoever is responsible for that ring of blue fire."

After breakfast she walked down the hill to where she and Helen had seen the strange phenomenon the night before. Here and there she found singed twigs and leaves, but had no time to look for other clues. Jim was waiting with the car.

When Nancy entered her own house a little later, she found Effie whistling cheerfully in the kitchen. Her hair was topped by a pink bow.

"Oh, hello, Nancy! Your father's gone already, but he said to tell you he'd see you tonight. Your friend Bess called. She and George are back. They want you to phone them right away."

Just then the back doorbell rang. Nancy opened the door to see a small boy standing there.

"Hello, Johnny," she said.

"Hi, Nancy!" he said. "What's in that box in your back garden?"

Effie cut in quickly, "A pigeon. And don't you touch it!" The girl explained to Nancy that she had taken the pigeon's box from the garage and placed it in the yard. I put on a lid with holes in it. Now he can get air and a little sunlight."

"I peeped through a hole," said Johnny, "and I saw something move. Is it a bird? I like birds. My Mummy has a parakeet. Oh, Nancy, can I have some biscuits?"

Nancy laughed and gave him the last one in the tin. "That's all."

"It's okay. I'll go play with your bird."

"No, no," Nancy said quickly. "Leave the bird alone. I don't want it to fly away."

The telephone rang and Nancy went to answer it. The caller wanted the library. "I'm sorry," Nancy said, "you have the wrong—"

She broke off as Effie's shrill cry sounded from the kitchen.

"Help, Nancy! The bird is loose!"

With a gasp of alarm, Nancy hung up the phone and dashed for the kitchen. Effie was standing at the back door, wringing her hands. Outside, Johnny was squatting beside the box, holding the lid in his hand. The pigeon was looking over the edge.

"Don't move, Johnny!" Nancy called, and hurried out with Effie behind her.

"He wants to fly," the little boy said. "He flaps his wings like anything. See?"

The bewildered bird hopped to the edge of the box and sat there, balancing and stretching.

"Stay still, Johnny!" Nancy warned. "Don't frighten it!"

"He isn't scared of me," the boy answered confidently. "He likes me. See?"

Johnny's chubby little hands swooped towards the

bird. Alarmed, the pigeon flapped its wings, rose awkwardly into the air, and landed just out of reach on a kitchen window-sill.

"Oh dear!" said Nancy, hardly daring to breathe. "We must get it down."

Effie was already dragging a light lawn chair to the window. "I'll get him for you."

"Wait! That won't hold you."

Before Nancy could stop her, Effie leaped on to the chair seat and reached for the sill. Nancy grabbed for the chair. Too late! It tipped. With a wild cry Effie toppled off, her arms flailing.

The frightened bird flew away!

·7

Unfriendly Keeper

"Effie! Are you hurt?" Nancy cried. But even as she helped the girl to her feet, Nancy's anxious glance went to the bird flying across the garden.

"I'm all right," Effie said breathlessly. "I'm sorry I scared him away. Oh, there he is!"

She pointed to the pigeon who had come to rest on the garage roof. Then, flying slowly and uncertainly, it flapped about in a circle and took off towards the front of the house.

Nancy grabbed Effie's hand. "Come on!" She pulled Effie towards her car, which was parked near the front door. "I'll drive. You watch for the bird. We must follow it!"

Flustered, Effie climbed in beside Nancy, taking off her apron and chattering apologies.

"Don't talk! Just watch," Nancy said crisply.

Effie, clutching her pink bow to keep it in place, gazed skyward. "There he goes!"

The pigeon was flying low along the street in front of the houses. Nancy started the engine and began to follow slowly.

"I don't think this will work," Effie said, "because we have to stay on the streets and the pigeon can fly in any direction."

"Maybe you're right," Nancy said grimly, "but we're going to try!"

"He's turning left," Effie announced. Quickly Nancy turned left into a side street and followed the bird until it veered again.

"Lucky he's flying low and slow," said Effie.

Now and then the bird fluttered to a rest on a roof or tree branch, but the girls managed to track it until they had reached open country beyond the suburbs of River Heights.

"My neck is stiff from watching," Effie said with a sigh. "Where's he going, anyway?"

"Home to its owner," Nancy replied. "Where is it now?"

"He went that way," said Effie, pointing across a field, "but I can't see him because of those trees."

"Oh, we mustn't lose it!" Nancy exclaimed. She stopped the car and scanned the sky.

Effie gulped. "I'm sorry. I can't see him. Oh, I could cry!'

"Well, don't," Nancy commanded. "That pigeon is one of my best clues. I must find it!"

Suddenly she spotted the large grey bird flying out of the clump of trees. "There he goes!" Nancy exclaimed.

Luckily the pigeon flew parallel to the road and Nancy drove along behind it.

"Please watch the bird, Effie," Nancy implored as her companion looked away.

"I'm not even blinking both eyes at once," Effie assured her. "I blink one eye at a time." After a mile, Effie suddenly pointed to a grove of elms that towered over the flat fields. "Look! He's going rourd and round over those trees. I think he's dizzy."

"No," Nancy said, and felt a quiver of excitement. "That's where it lives. I see buildings in the grove." A second later the pigeon disappeared amongst the trees.

Nancy halted the car beside a stone wall over which honeysuckle tumbled. A short distance ahead was a driveway.

"Listen, Effie," Nancy said firmly, "we are going in there and you are not to say a word about our keeping the pigeon or following it here."

Effie's eyes were wide. "Is there a gang of kidnappers in there?" she asked timidly.

"I don't know who's there," Nancy replied. "But we must be prepared for anything." Then, seeing thatEffie was trembling, she said, "Would you rather wait here?"

"Oh, no! I don't want to stay alone! But maybe I—I could hide in the boot."

They got out of the car and Effie scrambled into the luggage compartment. She left the lid open an inch so there would be fresh air.

Nancy slipped behind the wheel again and turned off the little-used, sandy road on to a well-kept gravel driveway. It swept in a great curve towards a long rambling white house.

Nancy drove nearly a quarter of a mile. Then the path dipped under the trees, and Nancy saw that the house was a mansion. Whoever occupied it must be very wealthy. White columns supported the overhanging roof of a porte-cochère.

The young sleuth did not stop there, but headed towards the outbuildings, to the far right of it. She pulled up in front of a stable.

Quietly Nancy got out of the car. Her sweeping glance took in a nearby shed and a large coop beside it containing a number of pigeons. On the roof rested the pigeon Nancy had been following.

The yard was empty. Except for the cooing and flutterings of the birds, the place was silent. Was it deserted? Nancy wondered.

Suddenly she was startled by a noise that sounded like a pistol shot. She whirled. In the shadow of the stable doorway stood a dark, thin-faced man wearing a riding habit. He carried a long, knotted, leather whip which he cracked again.

With an unpleasant grin, he said, "Scared you, didn't I?"

Keeping her voice cool and even, Nancy said, "Good morning. Is the owner here?"

"Nope," he said, studying her carefully. "What do you want?"

"I'd like to buy some pigeons," Nancy said.

"They'll be expensive," he said. "Ours are specially trained to fly both day and night. How many birds you want?"

"Two," Nancy replied. "Do you take care of these all by yourself?" she asked casually, hoping to get a lead on how many men worked at the place.

"Sure," he said. As he walked towards the coop, he spotted the pigeon on top of it. "Oh—oh!" he exclaimed softly. "So you finally got here!" He hurried over and picked up the pigeon.

The keeper looked it over curiously, then opened the capsule on the bird's leg. With sinking heart, Nancy remembered that the message was no longer there. She had intended to replace it before releasing the pigeon, but the bird's sudden escape had made this impossible.

When the man saw that the capsule was empty, he bit his lip and frowned. After putting the pigeon into the coop, he turned and walked back to Nancy, his eyes narrowing.

"It's a lovely house and grounds," she remarked innocently. "Who lives here?"

"I'm kind of busy this morning," he said curtly. "What kind of birds you want?"

"Any healthy pair will do," Nancy replied.

While they had been talking, the man's eyes had roved over the convertible and now he gazed at Nancy as if he were trying to make up his mind about something. Had he recognized her? Had Adam Thorne warned his accomplices to be on the lookout for her?

Suddenly the man said, "Okay. I'll get you a pair. You pay inside the house."

"Oh, no," Nancy thought. "I won't risk that. I think I'd better be ready to leave fast!"

As the pigeon keeper walked towards the coop, Nancy got back into the car and started the engine. Instantly he turned and hurried back.

"Hold it!" he said sharply. "I think you'd better come with me and pick out your own birds."

Nancy's heart began to thump. "No, thank you," she said coolly. "You can do it."

"Get out!" the man snarled and swiftly seized Nancy's arm with one hand. He tossed away the whip and reached into the car to turn off the engine.

Suddenly a weird sound came from the rear of the car. *Effie!* It sounded as if she was having an attack of hysterical giggles!

Startled, the man let go of Nancy's arm. "What's that?"

Instantly Nancy released the brake and roared off in reverse. In a shower of gravel she turned, then sped past the house and down the driveway. Fearing pursuit, she kept going for about three miles until she reached the small settlement of West Gramby. Here the young detective turned into the parking area of an old-fashioned timber-built hotel. Quickly she got out and raised the boot lid.

"Okay, Effie, you can come out now."

"Oh, Nancy, I'm sorry if I spoiled everything," said the red-faced girl as she jumped down. "When I heard that man order you to get out of the car, boy, was I scared! I wanted to scream, but all I could do was make a crazy laugh."

Nancy smiled. "Never mind. Your giggles saved the day."

To calm the excited girl, Nancy suggested that they have lunch in the hotel. While waiting for their order, Nancy phoned a neighbour of the Drews and asked her to give Hannah Gruen some lunch, and tell her that the girls would be home in an hour. Then Nancy questioned the hotel manager about the estate she had seen.

"The owner's name is Adolf Tooker," the man said, "and that's really all anybody knows about him. He's lived there a year or so, but he keeps to himself."

"Then he doesn't bother his neighbours?"

The hotel manager scowled. "His plane does, though, flying all hours of the day and night."

"Plane?" Nancy repeated.

"Little tan one, with a flying horse—or something—on the fuselage."

So she had been right! The pigeon had been released from the plane. Nancy was quietly elated, for she felt sure she had found the gang's hideout. But suddenly she remembered: *there were no larkspur!* And she had not seen a gate.

"The kidnappers must have two hideouts," Nancy decided. "The pigeons and the plane are used for messages and transportation between them."

When she and Effie reached home, they went at once to Hannah's room and told her about the pigeon incident. "You're having plenty of excitement, Nancy." The housekeeper sighed. "And here I am cooped up and no use at all!"

Nancy hugged her. "You've helped me so often you deserve a rest! And now I must call Bess and George."

When Bess heard about the invitation to the Cornings', she gave a whoop of delight. "Guess what?" she said. "I just finished talking to Dave. He and Burt are going to that very lake as camp supervisors. It happened suddenly, when three old supervisors dropped out. You'll probably hear from Ned soon. And now tell me more about the Cornings' mystery."

Nancy related it briefly, then phoned George. "I'll be ready whenever you say, Nancy."

Just before dinner that evening Nancy made up a bouquet of flowers from her garden and took it to the neighbour who had given Hannah lunch. On the way back, she noticed a black saloon parked across from the Drew house. Two men were seated in it with their hats pulled low. When they noticed her looking at them, the driver pulled away quickly.

"I wonder who they are," she mused.

Nancy unlocked the front door but could not push it

open. She tried harder. It still stuck. What had happened during her absence?

"Effie!" she called loudly through the crack.

In a few seconds an answer came. "Okay, I'll open it."

There was the sound of something heavy being dragged over the floor. Effie, pale and trembling, opened the door. "I put the living-room couch and a big chair here to keep those men out," she explained.

"What men?" Nancy asked.

"The ones in the car across the street. They—they tried to force their way in here, but I slammed the door in their faces."

"Good for you," said Nancy, both alarmed and amused. "Who were they?"

"I dunno."

"Well, they've gone, Effie, so don't worry."

Nancy herself was greatly concerned and peered from the window several times. The black saloon drove past every few minutes. It was not the one in which Dr Spire had been kidnapped. Just before Mr Drew arrived at dinner-time, the car parked once more in front of a house a few doors away. Nancy mentioned it to her father and asked if the police should be notified.

"Not yet," the lawyer said. "That would only scare them off. I want to find out what they're up to."

"I have an idea," said Nancy, and told him what had happened the night before and during the day. "The keeper passed along the pigeon story, of course, so they know I've seen one of their hideouts. And they probably suspect I have the note that was in the capsule. I think they tried to force their way in here to intimidate me so that I wouldn't call the police—or to take revenge on me if I had."

Mr Drew frowned. "Nancy, you are in great danger. You must get away—and secretly."

"Shall I go to the Cornings'?"

"Good idea."

"But how can I leave secretly, Dad?"

"I have the solution to that problem," he replied. "I'll give you my surprise present now."

·8·

Over the Wall!

"A surprise!" Nancy exclaimed. "How could that keep those men from following me?"

Her father smiled. "Can't you guess?"

Nancy's eyes suddenly sparkled. "Oh, I think I know. Dad, you didn't! It isn't!"

The lawyer laughed. "I did and it is. Your new convertible is at Packlin Motors. I was going to surprise you with it next week, but I'll have Mr French bring the car round as soon as it's dark outside."

"Oh, Dad, how wonderful!" said Nancy, hugging him. "You're the most generous father—" After a pause, she added. "Those men will be on the lookout for me in my old car and I'll be spinning off in a shiny new one!"

Then Nancy became serious. "I must leave here without their seeing me. You could have Mr French bring the new car to the street behind our house. I'll sneak out the back way."

"That's what I thought," said Mr Drew.

While he called Packlin Motors, Nancy hurried upstairs and told Hannah the news, then packed a suitcase for her visit at Sylvan Lake.

After dinner she called the Cornings to say she would be there later in the evening. Helen's grandmother was delighted.

At nine o'clock both the doorbell and the telephone rang at once. As Mr Drew headed for the door Nancy picked up the phone. Bess was calling to say that the cousins would meet her at the lake the next day. "Mother will drive us out. Sorry we can't leave now."

"That's okay."

When Nancy entered the living-room a muscular young man was talking to her father. She recognized him as Henry Durkin, security officer of the building where Mr Drew had his law office.

"Henry's going to help us, Nancy," her father explained as she walked into the room. "I called him while you were packing. Hannah can stay with her sister while you're away. Henry will drive her and Effie there after we've gone."

"Are you coming with me, Dad?" Nancy asked, surprised.

"I certainly am," he said firmly. "I'm taking no chances on your being alone if those men pick up your trail. After Henry takes Hannah and Effie, he will drive my car to the Cornings', pick me up, and take me to the airport. I have a conference in Chicago tomorrow and a reservation on the midnight plane."

Henry Durkin frowned. "Mr Drew, if I were you I'd call the police."

"That'll be your job as soon as Nancy and I leave the house," the lawyer said. "I don't want those men in the car disturbed until then. As long as they're parked on this street, we know where they are. Nancy," he added, "as soon as I reach the airport I'll call Lieutenant Mulligan and tell him about the Tooker estate. Now we must hurry."

While Henry Durkin brought Nancy's case downstairs, she rummaged in the back of her wall cupboard and found an old suitcase. She carried it to the hall below where her father was waiting.

"I have an idea, Dad. Suppose I take my old car out of the garage and park it at the kerb. If Mr Durkin carries this suitcase out and puts it in the luggage compartment, the men in the saloon will surely think I'm leaving in that car."

"Good," said Mr Drew. He switched on the porch light. "We'll make the front of the house as conspicuous as possible."

"And meanwhile," Nancy said with a smile, "we'll slip out the back door." When her car was in place she gave the empty bag to Henry. "Carry that as if it's full and heavy," she said with a chuckle.

As he went out of the door, Nancy stepped out on to the porch and called loudly and clearly, "Thanks a lot, Henry. Put it in the back."

Then she went inside and followed her father to the unlighted kitchen. He was carrying her case and his own. Together, they stepped outdoors and peered into the darkness. They wondered uneasily if there were any unseen watchers. Quietly they felt their way towards the rear of the garden.

Nancy was first to reach the high brick wall. With the help of the tough vines growing over it, she pulled herself to the top.

"Hand up the cases," she whispered.

Mr Drew did so and began to climb the wall. By now Nancy's eyes had become accustomed to the darkness and suddenly she saw a figure detach itself from the shadow of the garage and disappear down the driveway.

"Dad!" she whispered. "Someone was watching!"

"We must move fast then," he said, and dropped the cases to the ground in the adjoining back garden.

Nancy leaped down, landing lightly a moment before her father. Mr Drew grabbed the suitcases and they sped through the neighbour's garden, then down the driveway to the pavement.

At the kerb stood a beautiful convertible, its polished metal reflecting light from the street lamp several houses away. Despite their desperate hurry, Nancy felt a thrill of excitement.

"My new car!" she whispered.

As she reached it, a figure stepped from the shadows and her heart pounded. But a second later she relaxed.

"Here are the keys, Mr Drew," said a deep voice.

"Mr French!" exclaimed the lawyer as he tossed the two cases into the back seat. "Many thanks. Sorry we're in such a rush. Nancy's old car is in front of our house. The keys are inside. Will you pick it up? Nancy can come tomorrow and change licence number plates."

"How beautiful this is!" Nancy said.

She slipped into the driver's seat and turned on the ignition. A deep purr came from the engine. At the same time, the young sleuth glanced into the rear-view mirror and saw headlights sweep round the corner.

"I think they're coming!" she said.

The next instant her car was zipping forward. Nancy turned the corner and several more after that. Then she slid into a driveway and switched off the lights. A moment later the black saloon raced down the street and disappeared in the distance. Its licence plate was dangling so she could not read the number.

As Nancy gave a long sigh, Mr Drew patted her hand. "You certainly used your head that time."

"Thanks, Dad."

She enjoyed the drive to the lake, sensing the power of the new car. Finally she said, "I loved my old car, Dad. It did a good job for me, but this one is just marvellous."

"Glad you're pleased, Nancy. You certainly handle it like a professional."

At the lake the Cornings welcomed the Drews cordially. Over cool drinks, the elderly couple reported that Morgan had not returned, nor had the circle of blue i re i een seen that evening.

"We're still worried," their hostess said. "Mr Drew, it's kind of you to lend Nancy to us."

He grinned appreciatively at the implied compliment.

Presently Henry Durkin arrived. Mr Drew quickly said good night to the Cornings, kissed Nancy, cautioned her to be very careful, and left for the airport.

Shortly afterwards, Mrs Corning went with Nancy to the room with twin beds that she had occupied the night before. "Would you like your friends to be in here with you, Nancy?"

"It would be nice."

"Then we'll put in a divan tomorrow morning."

As Nancy unpacked, her thoughts turned to the missing servant. Since the fiery circle had not appeared after he vanished, possibly it had been a signal to Morgan to leave. But why?

"Did he go willingly?" Nancy wondered.

She hoped the next day would bring news of him. But there was no letter in the morning post nor a phone call. Nancy was inclined to think he had not left of his own volition, but had been forced to go.

Mrs Corning looked through her letters. "I have one from Brent's Department Store," she said. "A dress I ordered has come in. I'd like to pick it up."

Nancy quickly volunteered to take her to River Heights. "I must turn in the dealer's number plates on my car and get my own," she said. "Also, I have an errand at the jeweller's."

Helen's grandmother accepted the ride. While she was in Brent's, Nancy went to see if Mr Stone had learned anything about the crest on the gold bracelet.

"I was going to call you," the jeweller said, taking her into his office. "I heard from Abelard de Gotha today." Mr Stone handed Nancy a typewritten letter. "Read this."

"Dear Mr Stone:
The armorial bearings described in your letter are those of the Eldridge family, the crest dating back to Henry IV of England, and the quartering on the shield marking the union of the Eldridge house with the Gerrets in 1604.

At the time of the Louisiana Purchase, the New York branch of the family, consisting of Isaiah Eldridge, his wife Prudence and two children, received a large grant of land in what is now Missouri. I presume their descendants still live in or near St Louis, although I have no records to prove that.

Sincerely yours,
Abelard de Gotha"

"Does that help you in any way?" Mr Stone asked.

"Indeed it does," Nancy replied. "I'll try to contact any Eldridges in St Louis."

Nancy thanked the jeweller and hurried back to the car. Mrs Corning joined her a few minutes later. After new number plates had been put on the car, Nancy headed for the lake. When they reached the Cornings' home, Nancy went upstairs to leave her bag. As she opened the bedroom door, there was a cry of:

"Hi!" Bess and George rushed across the room and hugged her.

"Oh, Nancy, I'm so glad to see you!" Bess exclaimed.

George, with an affectionate grin, added, "You'd think we'd been separated for two years instead of two weeks!"

Bess was blonde, pretty, and somewhat plump. Her cousin George, a brunette with a short haircut and classic features, gave every indication of being a fine athlete.

"Nancy, I'm just bursting to tell you something," said Bess.

"No!" George protested quickly. "You promised not to breathe a word."

Bess gave a great sigh. "I don't know which is harder: to keep *on* a diet or keep *in* a secret."

Nancy laughed. "How long before you'll tell me?"

"This afternoon," said George, "you'll see for yourself."

"If I don't wither from curiosity first," Nancy said, chuckling.

After lunch Mrs Corning insisted that the girls sit on the beach to exchange news and take a swim. Though Nancy would have preferred working on the St Louis lead, she put her plans aside to please her hostess.

Presently the three visitors appeared in swim suits and beach jackets. Nancy's turquoise suit set off her smooth suntan perfectly, while Bess looked attractive in a butter-yellow costume. George was a trim contrast in sea green.

"How pretty you all are!" their hostess remarked. She led them down a back stairway, through the small store room next to Morgan's bedroom, and out to the gravel driveway.

"There's the way to the beach," she said, showing them a footpath which led into the woods.

As the three girls started down the path, George asked, "Where did you see the blue fire?"

Nancy pointed across the slope. "Near that end of the house."

"I hope I don't see it at all," muttered Bess.

Before long, they came out on a flat, narrow bit of shoreline a short distance from a jetty. A little girl of five was playing on the edge of it, while two women sunned themselves in beach chairs above the waterfront.

"Marie!" called one of the women. "Be careful!"

Nancy and her friends sat down on the jetty, enjoying the attractive scenery. A circling speedboat roared towards them. The girls realized that it was going to pass very close to the jetty.

Suddenly little Marie jumped up to wave. "Marie Eldridge!" cried the same woman. "Come here!"

Nancy was startled to hear the name Eldridge, but before she could question the child, Marie lost her balance and toppled into the water. The woman screamed and her companion cried out:

"The boat! It'll hit her!"

Nancy had already leaped to the end of the jetty. Without hesitation she dived in after the child, directly in the path of the oncoming boat!

·9·

Surprises

As Nancy hit the water the prow of the speedboat loomed overhead. Swiftly she put one arm round the floundering child, and placed the palm of her hand over Marie's face. At the same time Nancy plunged below.

Down, down, down! The little girl squirmed, but Nancy held her firmly. Looking up through the green water, she saw the black keel of the speedboat whiz past in a froth of bubbles.

Instantly Nancy shot to the surface. Barely thirty seconds had elapsed but it seemed like an eternity. Sunlight dazzled her eyes as the strong arms of Bess and George reached down and lifted the child to the jetty.

"Marie!" Nancy panted. "Is she—is she all right?"

"She'll be okay," said George as the child began to cry. "Marie has swallowed some of the lake, that's all."

By this time the two women had rushed over. "Mummy!" cried Marie. Mrs Eldridge scooped up her small daughter and hugged her.

"My baby!" the woman murmured. As she fondled the sobbing child she looked at Nancy. "How can I ever thank you?"

"Please don't," Nancy replied softly. "I'm so glad I was here."

"I want to do something for you," said the grateful woman. "I live in the white cottage at the north end of the lake."

Nancy smiled. "Perhaps you can, Mrs Eldridge. I would like to ask you something."

"Anything—anything," the woman said warmly. "Come and sit down."

She led the girls to the beach chairs and settled down comfortably with Marie on her lap. The little girl had stopped crying and cuddled up drowsily.

The girls introduced themselves, and Nancy said, "Tell me, are you from St Louis?"

The woman looked amazed. "Why, yes, I am. How did you know?"

"I've heard that an Eldridge family settled in Missouri many years ago," said Nancy. "They were originally from New York."

"That could have been my husband's people," the woman said, looking puzzled. "What's the matter?" she added quickly, for there was a strange half-smile on Nancy's face.

"I just can't believe it," Nancy said. "This must be my lucky day."

"What do you mean?" Mrs Eldridge asked.

"A short time ago," Nancy began, "under rather unusual circumstances, I came into possession of an old-fashioned gold bracelet with a coat of arms on it, which I traced. It belongs to the Eldridges."

"A gold bracelet!" the woman exclaimed, her cheeks flushing. "Was there an inscription on it?"

"'To my darling Mary from Joe'," Nancy replied.

The woman grew pale. "Where is the bracelet now?"

"Safe in my home in River Heights," Nancy replied reassuringly.

"It must belong to my husband's Aunt Mary!" Mrs Eldridge exclaimed. "How did you get it?"

As Nancy told the story, the woman listened intently, then said, "I must call my husband at once." She explained that he was in Richmond, Virginia, searching for his aunt.

"She has been missing since early spring. Our aunt is a very wealthy woman, rather eccentric at times. Several months ago she disappeared from her home, leaving a letter. It said she was on the verge of a nervous breakdown and was going to a hospital for a long rest. Aunt Mary asked us not to try finding her."

"I'm sure she is being held not far from here," Nancy said. "I, too, am trying to find her."

"And Nancy will!" George declared. She and Bess told Mrs Eldridge of their friend's success as an amateur detective.

"Miss Drew has already done me one great service," Mrs Eldridge said with a smile. She shifted the drowsy child to her shoulder and rose. "I can never thank you enough," she said as she started to leave.

Suddenly Mrs Eldridge stopped and looked back. "I forgot to tell you: Aunt Mary has a necklace which matches the bracelet. She wore the set almost constantly from the moment Uncle Joe gave it to her sixty years ago."

"I'm glad you told me," said Nancy. "It may be a helpful clue."

As Mrs Eldridge walked away, Nancy said to her friends "This has been a day of surprises!"

George grinned. "You haven't seen anything yet."

She pointed out to the lake. "Take a look at that!"

A long canoe with three young men was heading towards shore. A shrill whistle split the air as one of them waved.

"Ned!" exclaimed Nancy.

"And Burt and Dave!" Bess added. "That was our secret!"

"The boys called us last night," said George, "and when we told them we were coming here, they decided to paddle over today. Ned wanted to surprise you, Nancy."

"He certainly did and it's a grand surprise," she said with a broad smile.

The canoe grated ashore and the three athletic-looking boys jumped out. All wore dark-blue shorts with white shirts bearing the name *Camp Hiawatha.*

"Here we are!" husky, blond Burt Eddleton exclaimed with a grin. "The world's greatest camp supervisors!" He was George's special friend.

Dave Evans was a rangy boy with fair hair and green eyes.

Ned Nickerson, who was tall and handsome, grinned. "Now with us at the lake you girls can have some excitement!"

George and Bess burst into laughter and even Nancy had to chuckle.

"Nancy's way ahead of you today," said George.

"She usually is," Ned remarked. "Tell us about it. More mystery?"

"Two of them," said George. "And a rescue!"

Walking up the hill to the Cornings' house, Nancy told the boys all that had happened, passing lightly over the speedboat episode.

Ned gave a low whistle. "You're on two dangerous cases, I'm afraid, Nancy."

"Don't forget you can count on us," Burt said as they entered the store room.

Through an open door straight ahead they saw Mrs Corning in the kitchen. She was happy to meet the boys and at once invited the three couples to the yacht club dance across the lake the next night. "My husband and I belong and would love to have you accompany us as our guests."

"I'm sure we can get time off from our camp duties," said Ned. "We'll accept. Thank you."

Presently the boys said goodbye. "We have to get back to our young charges," Dave remarked. "See you tomorrow."

The girls dressed quickly and helped their hostess prepare a dinner of steak, potatoes, green beans, and melon. Afterwards, they insisted upon tidying the kitchen without her assistance.

It was twilight by the time they finished. Nancy excused herself and slipped out of the front door. Carrying a torch, she headed for the spot in the woods where she and Helen had seen the blue fire. After examining the singed leaves, Nancy concentrated on the ground beneath them. There were some bits of scorched brown wrapping paper. Picking them up, she wondered if they might help to explain the fire display. Nancy then hurried to her room and put the pieces away in an envelope.

"Maybe Ned can analyse them," she said to herself. "I'll check with him tomorrow night."

Though the group watched intently, the blue fire did not appear that evening. Before going to bed, Nancy told the Cornings that she was afraid Morgan might have been kidnapped. "Perhaps you ought to inform the police."

Mr Corning shook his head. "Morgan asked us not to," he said. "I'll give him another thirty-six hours."

Next day there was still no sign of the missing man-servant and Nancy asked for permission to search his room.

"Go right ahead," said Mrs Corning.

It was an attractive room with a large window over-looking the lake. Quickly and efficiently Nancy searched, but could find no clue to the man's where-abouts. She observed that the servant could leave the house by going through the store room and out of the side door without anyone seeing him.

"Has he a key to the doors?" Nancy asked Mrs Corning.

"Oh, yes. He usually came and went by the side door so he wouldn't bother us."

"Did he have many friends?" Nancy inquired.

"None that we know of. He was a quiet man and liked to stay by himself."

Nancy looked thoughtful. "The friendship card Morgan received makes me feel that an old acquaint-ance is after him for some reason. There may be a clue to this person in his references. If you still have them, may I examine the letters?"

Mrs Corning was not sure where the papers were. "I'll look for them tomorrow."

After lunch Nancy, Bess, and George drove to the eastern outskirts of River Heights to search for the larkspur house. They were riding along a shady country road. Nancy stopped in front of a small house where a woman was trimming the hedges. Under a nearby tree sat an old lady, shelling peas.

"Excuse me," said Nancy, "we're trying to find a large house in this area that has lots of larkpsur or bluebells round it. Do you know of such a place?"

"Can't say I do," the woman replied.

"What'd she say?" the old lady asked loudly.

"Nothing, Mother. Just some house they're looking for. She's deaf," the woman added to Nancy.

"I heard *that!*" the mother said tartly. "And I heard 'house' and 'bluebells'. They're lookin' for the bluebell house. And I know just where it is!"

· 10 ·

An Unwelcome Gift

"You girls listen to me!" the old lady shouted. "The house you want is over in the next township, just outside of Milford. Go right down Elm Road. You can't miss it."

The woman standing by the hedge shook her head. "I never heard you mention that place before, Mother."

The old lady's black eyes snapped. "I know lots I don't tell," she said.

The girls thanked the two women and drove off, excited at the lead. But as they neared the small town of Milford, Bess looked worried. "I'm beginning to wish I'd stayed home," she said. "I really don't want to meet any kidnappers."

"Now don't be a snob," George teased her cousin.

"It's all right for you to make jokes," Bess replied, "but I can't help it if I'm not brave like you two."

Nancy smiled. "I can remember times on some of my cases when you were way ahead of us."

"I surprised myself," Bess admitted.

Nancy spotted the sign marking Elm Road and turned into the narrow, treeless street.

"There it is!" exclaimed George. In the middle of the street was a garden full of bluebells.

"You mean there it *isn't*," Nancy said gloomily as

she pulled up in front of the white cottage. A faded sign BLUEBELL HOUSE hung by the door. "No mansion, no fence, no gate!"

"But whoever lives here must be interested in blue-bells," said Bess. "Maybe they could help you."

"Good idea," Nancy said, and the three girls went up the path to the door.

Their knock was answered by a thin, young woman wearing an apron. "Hello, girls," she said cheerfully. "I guess you want to see the china. Come on in!"

She walked quickly into a room off the hall, beckoning them to follow. Nancy tried to explain, but stopped short at the door of the room. Shelves and tables were filled with flowered china.

"All hand-painted," the girl said. "The prices are marked."

"Oh, how beautiful!" Bess exclaimed.

While she and George looked round, Nancy explained to the girl why they had called.

"There's no place like that around Milford," she said, "but have you tried the Brookdale section west of River Heights? I've heard there used to be lots of estates out that way."

Nancy thanked her and Bess bought three hand-painted cups and saucers.

"There's one for each of us," she said when they reached the car. "A souvenir of a wild-goose chase."

"It may not have been so hopeless after all," said Nancy, and repeated what the girl had said.

George looked thoughtful. "You told us Dr Spire rode about an hour to get to the house. Can't we narrow the search by going only to places that are about an hour from the road where the old saloon was parked?"

"We could," Nancy said. "But the chances are that the kidnappers drove a little longer than necessary just to confuse the doctor."

George grinned. "Nancy, you never miss a trick!"

A further search continued for some time but without success. Finally Bess reminded Nancy of the dance that night. "We'd better go home," she advised.

Hours later Nancy was seated with Ned on a bench outside the gaily lit porch of the yacht club. Lively music and singing came pulsing out from the wide open doors and windows.

"On a hunch I brought something for the chemistry expert," she said, and handed him the envelope containing the bits of paper she had picked up in the woods.

"I'm no expert," he protested. Ned's eyes filled with mischief. "You don't expect me to look at this, do you, when I could be looking at you?"

Nancy blushed and laughed. She was wearing a simple rose-coloured dance dress and her hair was piled high with a gardenia tucked in it.

"Please be serious," she said. "I have a hunch that the burning circle is made of fireworks which are carried by someone. I remembered that you once helped make a fireworks display at college."

Ned spilled the bits of paper into his palm. He looked at them carefully.

"Your hunch is right, Nancy. These are fragments of quickmatch."

"What's that?" she asked.

"The fuse which is used to light fireworks." He explained that it was a string coated with a mixture of gunpowder and glue and enclosed in a brown paper tube. "Then that's attached to the lances."

"And what are they?" Nancy queried.

"Paper tubes filled with chemical mixtures which burn different colours. The circle you saw is probably a wooden frame with long nails sticking out of it about an inch apart.

"The lances are forced upright on to the points of the nails. Then the quickmatch is nailed across the tops of the lances. It's rough to do," he added, "because the lances are very hard, and many times the nail goes into your finger instead. Well, does that help you?"

"Yes. If I can find out where the fireworks were bought and by whom, I may have a good lead."

The rest of the evening was pure fun and ended with supper on several of the members' yachts moored to the club's jetty. While taking the girls home, the three boys invited them to a swimming gala at the camp the next afternoon and the invitation was accepted.

By one o'clock the girls were ready for bed. Bess and George dropped off to sleep at once, but Nancy lay awake. Suddenly she sat up. There had been a noise downstairs. Quickly she put on her dressing-gown and slippers, then grabbed a torch from her suitcase.

Slipping past her sleeping friends, Nancy went quietly down the back stairs. At the bottom she heard a scraping sound in the store room.

Softly she opened the door and flashed on her light. Caught in the beam was a white-faced, frightened figure on his hands and knees. He looked up. The missing man!

"Morgan!" Nancy exclaimed. "What are you doing? Where have you been?"

"I—I dropped the door key," he stammered.

Nancy spotted the key and picked it up.

"Thank you. I was moving things, feeling around for it. Sorry I disturbed you."

"Morgan, we've been very worried about you," Nancy said. "Won't you please tell me what's wrong?"

"Nothing's wrong!" the man said quickly. "I'll explain in the morning."

He opened the door to his bedroom, stepped inside, and locked the door behind him. Nancy wondered if she should awaken her hostess to report the servant's return, but decided against this.

In the morning, before breakfast, Mrs Corning told the girls Morgan had already talked to her and her husband. She said he had begged forgiveness, and had told a rambling story about going to help a friend.

"I'm afraid it's not true, but we don't want to discharge him." She sighed, then said, "Here, I almost forgot."

She handed Nancy the names of the three persons who had written letters of recommendation for the manservant.

"If you don't mind," said Nancy, "I'll phone these men after breakfast."

An hour later she came down from the first-floor phone and reported to the Cornings in the living-room.

"Well, what did they say?" asked the old gentleman.

"None of these people have ever heard of Morgan." The couple sat thunderstruck.

"Then the letters were forged?" said Mrs Corning.

"I'm afraid so," Nancy told her.

"*Morgan!*" *Nancy exclaimed.* "*What are you doing?*"

"Impossible!" snorted Mr Corning. "I remember talking to one of those men on the telephone."

"You must have spoken to an impostor," said Nancy.

"But—but why would Morgan do this?" asked Mrs Corning.

"Maybe his past made it impossible for him to get recommendations any other way," said Nancy. "Whoever helped him must feel he has a hold over Morgan. Perhaps that is the 'friend' who has come back into his life."

Mrs Corning said presently, "Now that Morgan has returned, maybe it's all over."

"I doubt it," said Nancy. "He's still frightened."

Her host spoke up. "Morgan's always been honest and a hard worker. I say we give him another chance. Do you agree, Emily?"

His wife nodded. The girls said nothing.

After church and lunch Nancy looked through the advertising pages of the telephone directory for fireworks companies in the area, but found none. As she put the book away, there was a sharp knock on the front door. Nancy went to open it.

No one was there, but on the porch floor was a long, narrow parcel wrapped in brown paper. It was addressed to Morgan. Suspicious, Nancy went to tell the Cornings about it.

"Under the circumstances," she said, "would you like to open this before Morgan does?"

"No," her hostess said firmly. "I feel that what's Morgan's business is his business. Take the parcel to him, Nancy."

With misgivings, she carried the package to the

kitchen and handed it to the manservant. He stared at it and began to tremble. With shaking fingers Morgan removed the string and paper. He seemed lost in thought and unaware that Nancy was still in the room.

When Morgan opened the paper and saw the contents, his face turned white and he suddenly slumped to the floor.

In the package lay a few stalks of blue larkspur!

· 11 ·

A Hazardous Drop

QUICKLY Nancy knelt beside the unconscious servant.

"Morgan!" she said urgently, and lightly slapped his cheek. He did not stir. She wet a clean towel at the sink and patted his face.

A few moments later he moaned and muttered, "Last warning—tomorrow night—" Then his eyes opened and with Nancy's help he managed to sit up.

She called the others and while Mrs Corning telephoned the doctor, the girls assisted the man to his room. Mr Corning seated himself beside the bed, but Morgan would speak to no one.

In a short time Dr Bennett, an old friend of the family, arrived. He said that Morgan had suffered a slight heart attack, and ordered him kept quiet.

"That means no questions," Nancy thought. She had been mulling over the significance of the larkspur in the package. She put them in a vase. When the doctor had gone, she led the rest of the group into the living-room and told the whole story.

"Larkspur again!" exclaimed George. "I don't get it!"

"That's one of the clues in your other case, Nancy," Bess said, puzzled.

"Probably the two are connected," the young

sleuth replied. She told the Cornings briefly about Mary Eldridge.

Bess looked surprised. "Why, what could Morgan have to do with the old lady's kidnappers?"

"But Morgan has always been the soul of honesty," protested Mrs Corning.

"Perhaps not *always*," Nancy said gently. "I believe he may have a prison record—under another name, of course. It would explain why he needed forged recommendations. Now Adam Thorne wants repayment."

"Adam Thorne!" exclaimed George. "Why him?"

"Because all the years Morgan worked for the Cornings, no one bothered him, but after Adam Thorne broke out of prison, the friendship card arrived and the blue fire began."

Mr Corning stirred uneasily. "You spoke of repayment. What did you mean?"

"I think Thorne and his gang want to rob this house. Remember, the friendship card had no written message on it, but the picture showed a cottage with the door open."

"I see," said Bess. "That was the message—open the door."

Mrs Corning was pale. "Do you know when it is to be?"

"Tomorrow night, I think," replied Nancy. "I believe the larkspur was a signal to Morgan—his last chance to co-operate. Probably the gang showed the blue fire and abducted Morgan to intimidate him."

Mr Corning's face flushed with anger. "Scoundrels! We'll get the police at once!"

"Wait!" said Nancy. "This is only a theory. If we hold off until tomorrow night, we'll see if we're right. Maybe we can catch the thieves red-handed and solve both cases at once."

"But, in the meantime," George said worriedly, "Morgan may have told the gang where you are."

Nancy nodded. "Yes, I've thought of that."

When Mr Drew telephoned her a few minutes later he had disquieting news. The lawyer had reported to the police before flying to Chicago and asked them to keep in touch with him.

"Lieutenant Mulligan informed me they had not been able to trace the kidnap car. Also, when they arrived at the Tooker estate it was deserted. The gang had taken the pigeons."

"I understand, Dad. My visit forced them to run. They'll be more eager than ever to get me out of the picture."

An hour later Nancy, Ned and their friends were watching the swimming races at Camp Hiawatha. In the fun and excitement she found it hard to remember the threat of danger. Cheers and singing filled the air as the young campers put all their high-spirited enthusiasm into the contests.

When the swimming gala was over, she said, "It was great, Ned! Your little boys did so well!"

"Thanks," he said proudly. "Now we can go swimming. Burt, Dave and I have free time."

The boys showed their guests where to change into the costumes they had brought, then met them at the water's edge. Tons of ocean sand had been transported overland to make a beach for the camp. A float was moored a few rods from shore with a tower and spring-board for diving.

The three couples swam out to the float on which a dozen young people were frolicking. Ned introduced everyone.

"Oh, you're the detective," said one boy, playfully shielding his face with one arm.

Nancy laughed. "I promise not to delve into any of your secrets."

George called, "But watch out, my friend!"

Suddenly Ned asked, "How about a little diving?"

One by one the group went off the high board. Presently it became an impromptu gala.

"Nancy, show them that new one you just learned," Bess urged.

"I'll try." She smiled. "But I may flop."

As everyone watched, Nancy balanced upside down on the edge of the board for a breathtaking moment, then thrust herself off. Her body revolved in the air and straightened out so that her pointed toes cleaved the water like a knife. Down she plunged into the green waters of the lake, then bobbed to the surface to hear the cheers of the spectators.

"Wonderful! Perfect!"

Panting, Nancy climbed back on to the float. As she threw herself down in the sun to rest, Ned came over. "That was a beauty, Nancy."

"Just luck," she insisted.

Later, when Nancy swam ashore with her friends, she was met by Mr Dennis, the camp director. "Great diving exhibition, young lady! How would you like a job as a supervisor?"

"Thank you," Nancy said, smiling, "but I already have a job."

"Well, you and your friends stay to dinner," the man said cordially, "and the evening camp."

As he walked away, a bugle sounded. "We fellows must go now," said Dave, "but we'll take you home tonight after taps."

Nancy called Mrs Corning to tell her they would not be home for dinner, then the girls went to the guest dining-hall.

During the meal two small boys appeared at their table with their arms full of anoraks.

"Ned, Dave and Burt sent you their coats," piped the tallest.

" 'Cause you didn't bring yours," said the other. They put the jackets on an empty chair and fled as the girls thanked them.

It grew chilly after dinner and the trio were glad to put on the anoraks and pull up the hoods.

George flapped her dangling sleeves. "What a great fit this is!"

"Now you can't tell us apart," said Bess.

When it was dark, a long line of singing boys filed up a hill behind the camp. The girls followed their bobbing torches. At the top, the three stopped to look round. The wooded hill sloped steeply to a rocky cliff. Fifteen feet below it was a huge bonfire.

The girls watched the campers wind slowly down the path, and saw that the first ones were already seated on another slope to the far side of the fire.

"Come on," said Nancy, "but watch your step."

She went first, with George beside her and Bess on the right. As they picked their way downwards they could hear the giant blaze crackling.

Smoke billowed up and Bess paused, coughing. Suddenly a powerful push from behind knocked Bess off her feet.

Screaming, she began to roll down the hill towards the cliff and the leaping flames!

· 12 ·

The Crystal Garden

"BESS!" George exclaimed, horror-stricken. "She'll roll into the fire!"

Nancy scrambled down the hill, George beside her. With a flying leap she threw herself on Bess and stopped her from rolling. At the same time, George skidded down and caught one of her cousin's flailing arms. The girls lay gasping, only a few feet from the cliff and the bonfire below.

"Bess," Nancy whispered, "are you hurt?"

"N-no," Bess said shakily. "Oh, Nancy, somebody pushed me! If you and George hadn't . . ."

Nancy looked grim. "I think someone mistook you for me. And I don't want him to know he was wrong."

As she spoke, three supervisors hurried down the hill towards them, calling, "What happened? Anybody hurt?"

Nancy squeezed George's hand. "We'll pretend *I* am," she whispered, then closed her eyes.

"Yes," George called out. "Nancy Drew! Please hurry. I'm afraid it's bad."

"She's unconscious!" quavered Bess.

Moments later, a husky young man was carrying Nancy up the hill while one of his companions ran ahead for the camp doctor.

"And get Ned Nickerson," George called.

Forty minutes later Ned tenderly placed Nancy on the Cornings' living-room couch as Helen's grandmother closed the curtains.

"Okay," said Ned. "All clear." Only then did Nancy open her eyes and sit up.

"You're some actress, young lady," said Mr Corning.

Nancy smiled. "I didn't have to do anything. Ned and Bess and George were the real actors."

Bess giggled. "And the camp director and the doctor were good actors, too. Mr Dennis insisted that we use his station wagon to bring Nancy home."

"I just hope we fooled the one who pushed Bess," said Nancy.

"Morgan must have told the gang you were here," said George, "and one of them trailed us to the camp, waiting for the opportune moment to strike."

Ned frowned. "Someone probably is still watching this house. To make our act look really good, we ought to call the doctor for Nancy."

Mrs Corning hurried off to put in the call. Soon she returned, and she reported that Dr Bennett would be glad to co-operate.

Nancy chuckled. "We'll make the gang think I'm out of action. Then they'll pay no more attention to me and I can work freely."

George spoke up. "I have a suggestion. If someone *is* watching this house, he'll probably plan to speak to Morgan. How about Bess and me letting ourselves out the back door and watching?"

"I'll do it," Ned offered.

"No," Mr Corning said. "That would look too suspicious. I often take a little stroll outside before going to bed. In a few minutes one of you can follow me. While I'm out there no gangster will come to talk to Morgan through the window."

He waved aside objections and left the room.

His wife said worriedly, "Oh, I hope everything will be all right. But suppose they strike here tomorrow night?"

"I have a plan," Nancy replied, "if Ned, Burt and Dave will help us."

"Sure we will," said Ned. "It's not our night off, but I know three fellows who'll switch with us."

"The thieves probably will go for the safe," said Bess.

Mrs Corning shook her head. "I'm afraid they're after something very special. Come," she added, seeing the questioning expressions of her guests, "I'll show you."

As their hostess led the way down the hall, Nancy quietly outlined her plan to Ned. "I'll tell the others later."

Across the hall from the kitchen, Mrs Corning opened a door and flicked a wall switch. The room remained dark, but at the far side a tall glass cabinet lit up.

Bess gasped. "Oh ,how beautiful!" She and the others stared, amazed. Inside was a sparkling array of crystal flowers and butterfles set on shelves lined with black velvet.

"My husband gave me one on each of our wedding anniversaries," Mrs Corning explained as she led them to the case. "They are made in France. Each flower contains at least one valuable jewel."

Nancy noted a ruby glowing in the heart of a rose and a topaz set in a daffodil. The butterflies had diamonds for eyes.

"How could the thieves have heard about these?" George asked.

"My crystal garden was written up in a magazine some time ago," Mrs Corning replied.

Nancy examined the case carefully. "Do you have a key for this?"

Mrs Corning showed her a tiny gold one which she wore on a chain round her neck.

Just then the doctor arrived. He listened to the story of what had happened, then went to check on Morgan, who was much better.

When leaving, Dr Bennett called back through the open door for the benefit of any outside listener. "Miss Drew must remain in bed for at least forty-eight hours."

Ned followed the doctor and went to join Mr Corning. Inside the house Nancy said to her friends, "Dr Bennett played his part well." Then she told them her plans for the next day.

Half an hour later Mr Corning and Ned reported no prowler near Morgan's window. Ned said good night and returned to Camp Hiawatha.

Shortly before dawn, Nancy ate a light breakfast, then slipped into the garage and hid behind the front seat of her car. At eight o'clock the other girls came out with a picnic bag. George took the wheel and they drove off.

When she was sure they were not being followed, George pulled to the side of the road and Nancy took the driver's seat.

"Now for the larkspur house!" she said happily.

"But where is it?" Bess asked.

Nancy said that since the Tooker estate lay south-east of River Heights and the pigeon and aeroplane both flew over it, the other headquarters were probably to the north-west.

"I'll try that, anyway."

After a while the road narrowed and there were no houses to be seen. The countryside was generously sprinkled with patches of woodland and open fields.

The girls explored every side road. Most of these were merely forest trails which ended within a short distance. At other times the searchers found a cabin and inquired if there was a hospital in the neighbour-hood. The answer was always No, and again Nancy would go on.

Stopping only to eat a picnic lunch, the girls tra-velled all day, exploring the network of winding lanes. All three were tired, their nerves tense with the strain of being constantly on the alert.

Finally Nancy glanced at the clock on the dash-board. "Ten minutes past five," she said. "We'd better go back."

Nancy turned the car and began retracing the route to the main road. Suddenly she pressed down on the brake and they stopped short.

"Sorry," Nancy said, "but we just passed a sign that I didn't see when we drove along here before."

She backed a dozen feet and halted opposite a narrow dirt road. Nailed to a tree was a crude, hand-lettered board: L. S. LANE.

"What about it?" Bess asked. "That probably leads

to the cabin of a forest worker whose name is L. S. Lane."

"And on the other hand," said Nancy, "it could mean Larkspur Lane, and be a guide for the crooks."

"It's worth investigating," George remarked.

Nancy turned into the narrow roadway, wide enough for only one car. But here and there the side bank had been cut to allow a vehicle to park while another passed it.

Proceeding cautiously over ruts and bumps, Nancy presently pulled into one of the wider places on the right. She stopped the car close to the trees.

"This might be the right place, so we had better go on foot," Nancy said.

She led the way amongst the trees, keeping parallel with the road. The girls trudged through the underbrush for nearly a quarter of a mile but saw nothing unusual. The only sounds were the crackle of twigs breaking underfoot.

Suddenly Nancy halted. "Look!" she exclaimed softly. "Larkspur!"

A dozen yards ahead the trees ended. Just beyond was a high wire-mesh fence. Inside it grew a long border of exquisite tall larkspur.

To the girls' left a large gate across the lane shut off the entrance to the grounds. Next to it stood a small brown lodge.

"This is it!" Nancy whispered gleefully, and her friends nodded.

Beyond the gate the ground sloped gently. A gravel roadway led to the top of the rise, where a large white colonial dwelling with a broad veranda was visible amongst some trees.

"It's a beautiful place," Bess said in a low voice. "I can't believe crooks live here."

"We'll soon find out," said Nancy.

Cautiously the three girls moved forward, taking advantage of every tree trunk and bush for concealment. There was no sign of habitation. If anyone was inside the gate-house, he was not to be seen at the moment. Then, for an instant, a flash of white appeared in the distance near the brow of the hill.

"Did you see that?" George whispered tensely. "I'm sure it was a nurse's uniform."

"Listen! Do you hear a plane?" Nancy asked.

The girls peered upwards. Several minutes passed before the aircraft became visible. Then it shot overhead, flying low.

"It's the same type of plane that wounded the bird!" Nancy said quickly. "And it's like the one the hotel manager said flew into the Tooker estate. . . . Yes, there is that flying horse on the fuselage. This *is* the place!"

"Sure enough," said George. "Down he goes. The landing field must be behind the house."

The plane dipped low, lost altitude rapidly, and vanished behind the roof of the mansion.

"Now what do we do?" Bess asked.

"There is only one thing left," Nancy answered. "Somehow we must get inside!"

·13·

Baiting a Thief

GEORGE frowned. "You're not going to try getting into this place now, are you?"

"No," said Nancy. "I'd probably end up a prisoner." She thought of the old lady who was being held against her will.

"It's getting late," Bess put in. "We'd better go back to the Cornings'."

"Yes," Nancy agreed reluctantly. "We have our work cut out for us tonight."

"Why don't you just tell the police where the hospital is?" Bess asked nervously. "Let them rescue Mrs Eldridge."

Nancy shook her head. "We must get her to safety before the police raid starts. Otherwise, the gang might harm the poor woman to keep her from talking. We'll have to find out exactly where they're keeping her prisoner in the mansion."

"It's such a big house," Bess said gloomily, "Mrs Eldridge might be hard to find."

"It's also possible she's not here any more," George said. "The gang knows the police are after them and they may have moved her."

When they reached the car, Nancy hid in the back again and George drove. At the Cornings' Bess was asked to go in first and make sure Morgan was in his room.

"No use having him learn my secret," Nancy remarked. "Thorne might get it out of him before I'm ready to have it known." Learning the coast was clear, she scooted up to her room.

Mrs Corning had dinner ready, so a tray was prepared for Nancy. The others ate in the dining-room, then went upstairs.

"Now tell us your plan for capturing the thieves if they come," Mr Corning urged.

Nancy said, "Here it is. First, remember that the crystal-garden room has two doors—one to the hall, the other to the TV room. Each has a key that's now on the inside."

Her host nodded.

Nancy went on, "The boys will be outside. Dave will be watching in the shrubs bordering the flagstone area; Burt, at the top of the patch which leads to the jetty; and Ned, on the garage roof.

"As soon as the thief—or thieves—enters the house, Ned will signal with a walkie-talkie to Mr Dennis at the camp and he will call the police. Meanwhile, Burt and Dave will be ready to tackle anybody watching on the outside. We girls will lock any intruders in the crystal room."

"But suppose they see you?" Mrs Corning asked.

"They won't," said Nancy. "Bess and George will hide across the hall in the kitchen. I'll be in the TV room. As soon as the thieves enter, I'll lock the adjoining door. At the same time, the girls will slip across the hall and quietly lock that door."

Mr Corning asked what he and his wife should do.

"I suggest you go to your room as usual," Nancy replied. "That will cause less suspicion."

At nine o'clock the lights were put out on the ground floor, the couple retired, and the girls took their posts. Nancy held the door to the crystal room open a crack, put the key on the outside of the lock, and watched. It seemed that she stood for ages before the other door opened.

There was a *click* and the light went on in the glass cabinet. Nancy gripped the key, ready to shut the door. Suddenly she froze. Only one figure approached the cabinet.

Morgan! A thief!

He was carrying a large suitcase, which he put on the floor. Nancy watched, hardly daring to breathe, as he took a small tool from his pocket and picked at the cabinet lock.

A few minutes later he pulled the glass door open. Then he swung back the lid of the suitcase. Nancy saw that it was divided into compartments and heavily padded with velvet.

"A special carrying case," she thought.

As the man's trembling hands reached towards a fragile crystal flower, he suddenly drew back.

"No!" he whispered hoarsely. "I can't do it!" He buried his face in his hands with a sob.

Nancy hurried to his side. "Morgan!" she said softly. The man whirled and gave a gasp.

"Don't be afraid," she said quickly. "Let me help you."

He groaned and sank into a chair beside the cabinet. "How can you know—all this?"

"I know part of it," she replied. "Where is the gang? You were to let them in, weren't you?"

The thief pulled the glass door open

The man stared at her, amazed.

"Yes, but Thorne changed his mind. He said I should steal the crystal flowers and deliver them in this special case he gave me. I used to be pretty good at lock picking," he added, flushing miserably.

"That's how Thorne got his hold over you, isn't it?" asked Nancy. "He knew you'd been in prison and he helped forge your references."

The servant nodded. "I wanted to go straight and I did. I wouldn't hurt the Cornings for anything. But Thorne—he wouldn't leave me alone. Kidnapped me. Held me on a big estate. Said the larkspur would be the signal for this theft. I'd have to deliver—or else."

"There's a Mrs Eldridge being held prisoner there, too," said Nancy. "Did you see her?"

"Eldridge?" Morgan repeated. "I think I heard the name, but—" Suddenly he broke off. "Listen! There they are!"

The sound of a low whistle came from outside. Nancy flew to the switch and snapped off the light in the crystal case.

"I'll close it," Morgan whispered. The door clicked shut. "What—what shall I do?" he stammered.

"Listen," Nancy said quickly. "We'll have to get them in here. I have a trap set, but you must go out and tell the men you need help—that you're too weak to carry all the loot."

"They'd never believe me. I'm no good at acting."

"There must be some way to get them in here," Nancy declared. "Suppose you just don't go out."

Morgan gave a bitter laugh. "They'll go away. And in a day or so I'll disappear and never come back. Thorne will see to that. He won't stand for any double-cross."

Nancy had an idea. "Come with me!" She led the way into the hall.

At once the kitchen door opened. "What's up? George whispered. "Where's the gang?"

Nancy drew Morgan into the dark kitchen and explained to the girls. "But I've thought of a way to lure the gang into the house," she said. "If they find out I wasn't injured and am still working on this case, they'll come after me."

Bess caught her breath. "You don't mean you'd let them know?"

"Morgan will tell them," said Nancy. "Bess, you stay here and George will take over the door of the TV room. I'll go out with Morgan. If they don't believe him, I'll let them see me and then run in here. That should do it."

"No!" said the servant. "I won't let you, Miss Drew. Adam Thorne is dangerous. He will stop at nothing. It's too big a risk for you."

"I'm not afraid," said Nancy.

Suddenly Morgan darted away and ran through the store room. Nancy dashed after him, calling:

"Morgan! Come back!"

"No!" he called. "I'm telling Thorne, I won't do it. I don't care what happens to me!"

Nancy raced outside and grasped the panting man.

"Thorne," he called, "I won't do it!"

"Morgan!" Nancy cried frantically. "Come inside!"

An instant later powerful hands gripped Nancy's shoulders and swung her away from Morgan. She reeled and fell backwards in the darkness. Nancy struck the gravel driveway hard and blacked out.

· 14 ·

The Matching Necklace

As NANCY's eyes fluttered open, she saw Bess's anxious face bending over her.

"Oh, thank goodness!" Bess exclaimed. "She's coming to."

George and Mrs Corning stood at the other side of the bed. "You're in your room, dear," said Mrs Corning. "How do you feel?"

Nancy sat up, frowning. "My head aches, but otherwise I'm all right. What happened?"

"The boys found you on the driveway," said George. "The gang got away." She explained that the boys had seen three men scuffling and finally one had been carried off through the woods. By the time the boys had rescued Nancy, their search for the others was hopeless.

"They took Morgan, then?" Nancy asked. "I was afraid of that." She told how she had been pulled away from him.

"Lucky the thug didn't know it was you," said George, "or you'd have been kidnapped, too."

"The boys are waiting in the kitchen," Bess put in. "I'll go down and tell them you're awake."

"Let's all go," said Nancy. "I think I could do with

a glass of milk and something to eat, if you don't mind, Mrs Corning."

The woman's face broke into a smile and she said, "That's the best news I've heard yet. Now I know you're feeling better."

As Bess and George served cake and glasses of milk, Nancy and the boys exchanged stories.

Dave raised his glass of milk. "Here's to General Drew!"

The others echoed the toast enthusiastically.

"I guess I wasn't such a good general tonight," said Nancy. "I certainly lost the battle."

"The campaign's not over," Burt told her cheerfully.

Ned smiled and patted Nancy's shoulder. "Better luck tomorrow."

Mrs Corning cleared her throat. "Nancy, dear, I'm afraid we had better—"

"Oh please, Mrs Corning! I know what you're going to say—that I'd better give up the case. But please give me another day to find out exactly what's going on at Larkspur Lane."

Ned and the others backed up Nancy's plea.

Mrs Corning hesitated. "Well, all right, but we can't wait longer than tomorrow night."

"I'll do my best to solve the mystery by then," Nancy said quietly. To herself she added, "And no mistakes, Nancy Drew!"

Next morning the girls again started out early. As before, Nancy hid in the back of the car and George drove. The sky was overcast, but Nancy's spirits were light. Some miles from the lake she took the wheel, her eyes shining with excitement.

"I don't see how you can be so cheerful," Bess grumbled. "You were knocked out last night and now you're going into more danger."

Nancy smiled. "I never felt better."

Familiar with the way now, she was able to make good time to the spot where the sign "L. S. LANE" marked the battle line.

"We're in enemy territory now," she remarked. "From now on, caution must be *our* password."

Nancy drove past the half-concealed driveway and into the woods, where she parked the car behind a tangle of creeper and bitter-sweet.

"No one will notice it here," Nancy said. "Now let's start through the woods ahead and see how close we can come to the house without using the road."

Cautiously the girls worked their way round bramble and bush until the roof of the gate-house came into view. They crept closer and looks of dismay came over their faces.

Tilted back in a chair against the gate-post was a man whom Nancy assumed was the gate-keeper. At his feet lay a brindled Great Dane, his tongue lolling and his eyes alert

Nancy gasped. "That's the beast that tackled me at the flower show!" she whispered. "Let's hope he doesn't scent us."

George said, "There's certainly no chance of getting in here. Let's go on!"

Nancy led the way to the right, still well within the trees, always keeping the tall fence with its border of larkspur in view. After trudging through the woods for a quarter of a mile the girls found that the fence turned to the left. It continued in a straight line up the shallow slope along the flower-lined enclosure.

"Ugh, it's rough travelling," Bess shuddered. "I'm afraid of snakes."

"Want to wait here?" George asked.

"I certainly do not," Bess retorted. "I'd be scared to death by myself."

Smothering her fears, Bess followed Nancy and George through the tangled undergrowth. At one point they came to a place where a clump of trees partially concealed the house. Nancy called a halt for a rest and consultation. She and George sat down.

"This wouldn't be a good spot to climb the fence," George observed, leaning back on her elbows. "You'd rip your skirt on that barbed wire."

Nancy looked at her in surprise. "You'd do more than that! Don't you see?" she asked, pointing to the top of the enclosure.

"I see a fence and two strands of barbed wire stretched along the top," George replied.

"Notice how the wire is fastened to the supporting posts."

"It's attached to little porcelain knobs. What does that have to do with it?"

"Those knobs are insulators, which means the wire is charged with electricity. If you touch it, you will probably set off an alarm and get a bad shock besides. You could be killed."

George gave a low whistle.

"It's a regular fort," said Bess. "Yet how peaceful it all looks!"

Through the wire fence the girls could see other flower gardens, occasional clumps of trees, and a view of the rear of the gate-house. It was truly a lovely spot, except for the sinister strands of charged wire.

"Rested?" Nancy asked. "Let's go!"

Since they were now approaching the house, the girls moved even more warily. Bess stepped gingerly, afraid of putting her foot down on a snake.

"It would just be like those people to let a couple of thousand rattlesnakes and copperheads loose round here," Bess muttered. "Ugh," the worried girl cried suddenly, and jumped sideways, clutching at her cousin. Caught off balance, George stumbled and fell, giving a muffled yelp.

"What happened?" Nancy whispered excitedly, turning back to them.

"I stepped into a hole, and I—I think my ankle is sprained," George said, her face white.

Nancy's heart sank. If any of them should become helplessly injured, detection would certainly follow.

"Oh, it's all my fault," whispered Bess. "I'm sorry, George. I thought I stepped on something alive." Her eyes filled with tears.

George managed a grin. "Take it easy. I'm not dying."

Nancy knelt beside George, and with deft fingers felt the injured ankle, wishing that Dr Spire was with them now!

"I'm sure it's not broken," she said softly.

George rubbed her ankle gingerly. "Go on, you two. I'll wait for you here."

"Sure you're all right?" Nancy asked.

"Yes. Go on, please."

Nancy and Bess resumed their cautious advance to the top of the rise. There they had a full view of all the grounds.

Surrounding the house was a wide lawn with gravel walks and flower beds. In the rear was a huge meadow which Nancy surmised was used as a landing field for the aeroplane. The craft was not in sight.

Just below the brow of the hill, and connected with the house by a long arbour, was a group of outbuildings —a carriage house evidently converted into a garage, a good-sized barn, and a chicken yard.

"Listen," Nancy said, raising a finger. "I heard cooing."

"Pigeons!" Bess exclaimed.

The girls moved ahead until they were behind the carriage house, where they saw a small wooden building which had no window on their side. Here they rested in the shade until aroused by soft cooing and the sound of a man's voice.

"You're getting better!" the listeners heard through the wooden walls. "I guess you'll be able to work again if we keep you warm with this electric light. That'll cure you!"

There was more cooing. Then the unseen man said, "You ought to be ashamed taking a couple of days getting to the boss's place and arriving there lame at that! And why did you go to Drews', you half-witted barnyard goose?" A door closed and all was silent.

"Did you hear what that man said?" Bess asked with a catch in her voice. "He mentioned your name!"

"Yes. That was the man I met at Tooker's estate. I recognized his voice," Nancy said as she walked ahead.

Once past the outbuildings, the girls saw a moss-covered sundial surrounded by a grassy court. In it stood a number of wheel-chairs, each occupied by an old lady.

A large woman in a nurse's uniform had her back to the girls. She seemed to be administering to one of the elderly women.

"It looks like a real nursing home," Bess whispered. "Perhaps our suspicions are all wrong."

Nancy put a finger to her lips. The nurse turned and walked towards the fence.

"That's the woman who stole my handbag!" Nancy exclaimed softly.

"The one who took the bracelet?"

"Yes. She's in league with Thorne and Tooker, I feel sure."

"One of those old ladies may be Mrs Eldridge," Bess said, "but how can we find out?"

"I don't know yet, but I'll think of something," Nancy replied. "Meanwhile, we'd better go back and help George to the car. If she were discovered, she'd have no way to escape."

The girls hurried back to their companion and the three made their way down the hill. George limped along as quickly as she could, but progress was slow. When they had nearly reached the gate-house, the girls paused and George sat down on a stump to rest.

Suddenly Nancy seized Bess's arm and pointed amongst the trees. On the other side of the wire barrier was an old woman, dozing in a wheel-chair.

"Stay here," Nancy whispered. "I'm going closer."

Bess clung to her friend's arm. "No! Suppose they catch you!"

"I must talk to that old lady," said Nancy. "She may be able to help us."

Cautiously, Nancy crept towards the fence. When she was a few feet away, still screened by bushes, she stifled a gasp. The elderly lady wore a necklace which looked like the gold bracelet Dr Spire had given Nancy as a clue.

"The missing Mrs Eldridge!" Nancy murmured excitedly.

· 15 ·

Daring Plans

"Do I dare go closer?" Nancy wondered, watching the woman behind the fence.

Just then the old lady awakened and for a moment sat up straight in her wheel-chair.

"Oh dear!" she said. "I thought—I guess I dreamed I was—"

Her wrinkled chin twitched and she leaned back with closed eyes. Tears crept from under her lids.

Nancy was about to speak when she spotted a white figure hurrying down the hill. The nurse!

"So there you are!" she said harshly, drawing near the old woman. "I thought so! Trying to hide again!"

A sob escaped the elderly patient.

"Come now, stop that crying!" the nurse commanded. "If you act like a baby, you will have to be treated like one."

The old lady lifted a fragile, blue-veined hand in protest, but let it drop limply.

"Very well, Mistress Contrary, you may sit there for half an hour," the nurse snapped. "Lucky for you I'm tender-hearted, or I'd take some of your privileges away. See that you're here when I come back." She strode up the hill.

As the patient closed her eyes wearily, Nancy edged closer. "Mrs Eldridge! Mrs Eldridge!"

The old lady's eyes snapped open and she looked wildly about her.

"Here I am on the other side of the fence, behind the trees," Nancy said. "Listen closely, I will bring you help."

"How do you know my name? Who are you?" Mrs Eldridge whispered.

Nancy moved closer. Quickly she told the woman who she was, then explained how she had identified her.

Mrs Eldridge clasped her thin hands. "Bless you, child," she said, "but you can do nothing."

"Yes, we can," said Nancy, speaking with confidence. "But you must be brave and ready to follow instructions."

Bess and George had moved up to Nancy, who quickly introduced them.

"We'll all help you, Mrs Eldridge," Bess said.

"You can trust Nancy." George spoke cheerfully, despite the pain in her ankle.

The old woman smiled. "What brave young girls!" Her chin lifted and a glint came into her eyes. "All right. I'll do my part."

Nancy glanced uneasily up the hill. "We'd better stay out of sight while we're talking."

The girls stepped back and crouched down behind the bushes. "Tell us where your room is," Bess urged. "We'll get you out, then call the police and they can rush the place."

"No, no!" exclaimed Mrs Eldridge. "We've all been warned that if strangers try to enter the grounds, we'll be locked in the cellar."

"The police would find you," George said.

"Yes, but some of the women here are heart cases. Many of them could not stand the shock. Hush! Dr Bell is coming!"

"Bell!" thought Nancy, recalling the bluebell code message.

Quickly the girls slipped back amongst the trees and watched. Striding down the slope was a tall, distinguished-looking man in a black suit. He had smooth grey hair and a pointed beard.

He spoke in honeyed tones to the old woman. "Well, well, what has upset our dear patient?" he asked, bending over and gallantly kissing her hand. "I'm afraid you fret too much. However, I must tell Miss Tyson to be less strict with our favourite guest. Shall I call Luther and have him wheel you through the gardens?"

"No, just leave me alone," Mrs Eldridge sighed.

"Yes, that is what you need—rest and quiet," Dr Bell agreed. "But," he went on, "we must talk business. Shall we get that little matter of signing the transfer papers over now?"

"Your proposition is nothing short of robbery, and I will not consent," Mrs Eldridge replied, sitting bolt upright.

"Dear me, how harsh you are," Dr Bell said soothingly. "When you came here, you had every confidence in me. You entered this place of your own accord. You didn't give your relatives any idea where you were going. Didn't you agree to that as part of your treatment?"

"Fool that I was, yes!" snapped Mrs Eldridge. "But you haven't kept your part of the bargain to me or to any of the other ladies. You promised a special secret treatment—so secret you don't want anybody to know about it. That's why you have this isolated place."

"The special treatment to restore youthful vigour isn't ready yet," Dr Bell replied. "But it will be very expensive. I must have the extra money now."

"Oh!" Nancy thought. "He's undoubtedly a fraud!"

"I demand that you let me go," Mrs Eldridge cried out.

"We can't do that," Dr Bell said. "It would discredit our hospital to have a person leave in a poor state of health. Besides, I have your signed declaration that you are a patient here of your own accord, and that you agree to remain as long as I think necessary. Naturally, I forbid you to go."

Mrs Eldridge glanced quickly towards the woods where the girls were concealed. In a loud, clear voice, she said, "You wish me to sign over to you many thousands of dollars, in addition to the three thousand I have already paid you".

"And why not?" Dr Bell retorted irritably. "There are other patients whom I have charged more."

"Well, I suppose that once the papers are signed, I won't live very long," the old lady said meaningfully.

"You will feel like a girl again," Dr Bell replied.

"I'd rather live without youthful vigour and be out of here!" Mrs Eldridge said, closing her eyes. "I won't sign a thing. If you should kill me, you won't get a cent. That's all. I wish you would go. I am very tired."

Nancy saw the doctor's face turn red. His beard seemed to bristle, and his eyes blazed with rage.

"You'll sing a different tune if you don't do as I say," he fumed. "I've wasted enough time on you. I will give you until nine o'clock tonight to come to your senses!"

"Oh, you are a brute," Mrs Eldridge cried. "If only some good angel would come to my little room in that hot south corner on the third floor and rescue me!"

"Say, what are you talking about?" Dr Bell asked, looking about him suspiciously. "You don't think any angels are listening to your careful directions, do you?"

The girls could not help grinning.

Dr Bell turned and shouted, "Luther!" A man in a white uniform came out of the gate-house. "Take Mrs Eldridge to the porch!" the doctor snapped. "Any word about the new patient?"

"A message arrived by Bird X that she will be here at nine," the attendant said with a wink as he wheeled Mrs Eldridge away.

Swiftly, the girls made their way towards the car. Nancy took the wheel and headed for the main road. As they drove along, the sun broke through the overcast sky.

"We're going to Glenville," she said. "It's about five miles from here. George can see a doctor there."

"What about Mrs Eldridge?" Bess asked.

"No plan yet," Nancy said tersely, "but I'm thinking."

Her companions asked no more questions. When they reached the small town, Bess went with George, while Nancy telephoned Ned from a telephone kiosk. She told him what had happened and alerted him to his part in the plan she had devised.

"You can count on me," he said.

An hour later the girls met in a coffee bar for a late lunch. "My ankle isn't sprained," George reported. "The doctor put on a bandage and it feels better."

"Good," said Nancy. "Are you ready for danger?" she asked soberly.

"Of course we are," George answered steadily.

"Anything to get those poor old ladies free and home to their families," Bess added.

"Then right after we eat, I'm going shopping, while you two hire a black saloon. You may have to drive to another town for it, so let's meet here about five. Then I'll tell you the plan."

At the appointed time Nancy came hurrying down the street, her arms filled with packages. Bess and George were waiting in Nancy's convertible behind which stood a black saloon parked at the kerb.

"What did you buy?" George asked in amazement.

Nancy grinned. "Black shoes, a black hat with a heavy veil, grey gloves, and a long black coat much too big for me!"

George's eyes grew wide. "Nancy! You're going to dress up like an old lady!"

"That's right. I'll be that new patient who is supposed to arrive at nine o'clock. Only I'll be there early."

Bess stared at the parcels Nancy was holding. "What's in that fifth bag?"

"A nurse's uniform and a pair of horn-rimmed glasses for you," said Nancy.

Bess gasped. "Me?"

"Yes. You'll have to drive the car into the hospital grounds," Nancy replied.

"Oh, my goodness," was all Bess could say.

Immediately George offered to go instead, but Nancy said No. "You never can tell what will happen." she said. "With that bad ankle, you wouldn't be able to run if it should be necessary."

Nancy put the packages in the convertible's boot and suggested that they eat tea. They found a small restaurant on a side street and ordered sandwiches and coffee.

"What's my part in the plan?" George asked.

"I want you to stay with the convertible—in the clearing where we hid it before," Nancy said. "Bess may need your help when she brings Mrs Eldridge out."

George nodded. "I see. I'll play it cool."

"But what about you, Nancy?" asked Bess. "You're not going to stay in that awful place?"

"Yes. We must get Mrs Eldridge out before nine o'clock. After that, I'll give the signal for the rescue of the others. A pigeon will carry it to the deserted Tooker estate where Ned is stationed."

Nancy glanced at her watch. "There's no more time to talk now. We must get started."

With George driving the convertible and Nancy the saloon, they returned to the clearing near Larkspur Lane. There Bess changed into the nurse's uniform and Nancy put her costume over her own clothes.

Bess, wearing horn-rimmed glasses, looked stern in her white uniform and cap. Nancy seemed small and frail in the long black coat and heavily veiled hat.

"I'd never know you," George exclaimed.

Ten minutes later in the gathering dusk, the saloon reached the gate-house.

"Now remember to give the password," Nancy whispered.

Trembling, Bess halted the car in front of the gates as the gate-keeper appeared and chained his Great Dane securely. The huge dog strained at his leash and barked furiously. His master advanced towards the girls.

Suppose the password has been changed?" Nancy thought fearfully.

"What's the good word?" demanded the watchman hoarsely, stepping closer.

"Singing horses!" Bess whispered, quaking.

· 16 ·

Sleuthing

"SINGING horses," repeated the guard. "Right you are."

Striding up to the gates, he opened them wide. Bess guided the car between the posts and the portals clanged shut behind them.

The password had permitted them to enter!

Both girls heaved sighs of relief as they sped up the gravel driveway. Halfway to the mansion, Nancy spoke.

"Stop. No one can see us from the house yet, and the lodge is concealed by those shrubs."

Bess brought the car to a halt and Nancy said, "Back the car off the drive into that clump of trees, Bess. Good! Lucky there's enough room. Get in as far as you can. Keep on backing—farther. That's fine! Now, you wait here. I'll return as soon as I can!"

"Don't be too long," said Bess, trying not to sound frightened.

Nancy squeezed her friend's hand and slipped out of the car. As she went up the hill, she could hear the dog down at the gate-house growling.

"I hope he's still chained," she thought.

Near the mansion, Nancy assumed a stooped posture and uncertain walk.

"I must be on my guard," she told herself.

Light streamed out on to the lawn from the windows of the house. Staying in the shadows, Nancy reached the walls of the mansion and made her way round to the back where she found an open door.

Peering through, she saw a wide, dimly-lit hallway with stairs ascending to her left, and guessed that this was a back door to the main corridor.

"Now for a trip inside," she murmured. "I hope my new shoes don't squeak."

Quietly she stepped into the hall. Half-a-dozen wheel-chairs stood about. Two of them had sleeping occupants, but there was no other sign of life.

Nancy moved on tiptoe towards the broad stairway, and had just reached the steps when she heard the tread of feet on the wooden floor. In a flash she darted to an empty wheel-chair, and muffled herself in the light woollen blanket left by its last occupant.

"I'll try to look as if I'm asleep," she thought.

At that moment a young woman in a striped uniform entered the hall. Nancy watched her apprehensively, fearing that the hat and veil would excite some comment. The nurse's helper, however, marched by humming to herself, giving none of the chairs a second glance.

As soon as she disappeared through a door, Nancy leaped up and dashed towards the stairs. A white head poked up from the nearest chair, and a cracked voice cried:

"Hi there, my dear. The doctor seems to have more than cured you. Why, you are young again!"

Nancy did not pause, but with hammering heart ran up the steps to the first floor. She glanced quickly round, then started the climb to the next storey.

At the top of the stairs, she peered cautiously down the corridor. Empty! Relieved, Nancy tried to get her bearings.

"The south corner room," Mrs Eldridge had said. "That would be to my right."

Quickly Nancy tiptoed down the hall and stopped before the last door. She bent to look through the key-hole, but could see nothing. Then she turned the knob.

The door was locked!

As Nancy racked her brains to think of a way to open it, she heard footsteps on the stairs. She darted across the hall and tried the handle of the opposite door. It turned, and she stumbled into total darkness. It was not a room, but a small broom cupboard.

It was a tight squeeze. Nancy did not dare move, for in the brief moment that the door cupboard was open, she had seen that the floor was filled with pails. Against the wall were mops, brooms, and other cleaning equipment. Her slightest movement would send them clattering to the floor.

With her ear to the door, Nancy waited. The footsteps approached, coming her way. They stopped outside her hiding-place!

For an instant she dared not breathe. Then there was the rattle of a key in a lock, and the clink of china on a tray. Nancy guessed that a bedtime snack was being brought to Mrs Eldridge.

Cautiously she opened the door and saw a white skirt vanish into Mrs Eldridge's room. Then came Miss Tyson's harsh voice.

"Wake up, Mrs Eldridge! Here is your medicine and some food. If you don't do as the doctor says, it will be the last snack you'll taste for a long time!"

The patient groaned faintly, and the nurse went on speaking.

"I have some nice hot consommé and toast and rice pudding. Doesn't that make your mouth water? Taste it, and remember that tomorrow there will be only stale bread and warm water for breakfast, lunch, and dinner if you don't obey our dear good Dr Bell, who is so kind to you."

An idea suddenly occurred to Nancy. "If that nurse is going to lecture Mrs Eldridge, I'll have some time to act," she decided.

Swiftly Nancy tore a strip from her veil and slipped out of the cupboard to the opposite door. It stood slightly ajar.

With the piece of net, Nancy plugged the slot in the door frame into which the bolt of the spring lock fitted. Then she darted back to her hiding-place.

"I hope my scheme works," she thought.

As Nancy stepped back and pulled the door shut, she bumped against a broom. The handle fell forward. Quickly Nancy caught it and another broom which toppled.

For a moment she clutched the wooden handles in the dark, her heart pounding. Then, very cautiously, Nancy propped them against the wall again.

"Oo! That's all I need!" she murmured. "One noise and I'll be trapped!"

Miss Tyson remained to threaten Mrs Eldridge a few minutes more, then left the room. She closed the door, and apparently thinking it was locked, hurried away.

Nancy listened for her to go downstairs, then ran to the door across the hall. Her trick had worked! The bolt had failed to lock! Nancy pushed the door open and stepped into the room.

"Mrs Eldridge," she said softly.

The old lady was propped up in bed, with two pillows behind her back, contemplating her bed-time snack. With a sigh she pushed aside the tray on her lap.

"Mrs Eldridge," Nancy whispered again, coming closer to the elderly woman.

The patient looked up and gave a sharp scream. Nancy flew to her side. "Don't be afraid! It's Nancy Drew, the girl who spoke to you through the fence," she whispered, quickly lifting the veil.

"I'm sorry! I—I'm nervous," the old woman gasped. "They have tried their best to frighten me so often. How in the world did you get in?"

"Don't worry about that. The thing to do now is for you to get out of here. I hope ho one heard you scream." But as she spoke, she heard someone running down the hall.

"I heard Mrs Eldridge scream," came Miss Tyson's voice.

"What of it?" said a second speaker.

"I suppose I'll have to chase into her room again," the nurse said irritably.

"I wouldn't bother," came another voice.

"But I can't let anything happen to her," said the nurse.

"She hasn't signed yet?"

"No."

Nancy looked round the room. There was not even a clothes cupboard to hide in!

Mrs Eldridge groaned. "Oh child! What will you do?"

As the doorknob turned, Nancy dived under the bed. It was very dusty there and she lay motionless, almost afraid to breathe.

Nancy saw a pair of white leather-shod feet stride into the room and pause at the foot of the bed, a few inches from her nose.

"You screamed!" Miss Tyson said angrily. "Why, Mrs Eldridge?"

"Oh, did I?" the patient asked in a weak voice. "I am sorry."

"Whether you are sorry or not makes no difference!" Miss Tyson snapped. "There are other patients in the house whom you upset by carrying on in that way. Why did you scream?"

"I am really very sorry," Mrs Eldridge said, trying to find some excuse for her outcry. "It won't happen again."

"I asked you why," the nurse said sharply.

There was no reply.

"Answer my question!" exclaimed the nurse, stamping her foot and raising a cloud of dust. Nancy pressed the hat veil to her face, trying not to sneeze.

"The—the consommé is very hot," Mrs Eldridge said. "It burned my tongue."

"A likely story." The nurse sniffed. "The broth is not as hot as all that after being carried up from the kitchen. No, that is not the truth, Mrs Eldridge, and I intend to find out your real reason."

"Oh, Miss Tyson," begged the patient, "don't scold me."

"I had to make a special trip up here on your account."

"That's too bad. I'm sorry."

"Well, why did you scream? What have you been doing?" rasped the nurse.

"Nothing," replied the old lady. "I haven't been out of bed."

"You've been acting strangely ever since this afternoon. You're up to something! Then the nurse added in a bullying tone, "You know what I'm going to do?"

"What?" asked Mrs Eldridge.

"Search this room!"

Attic Hideout

AT THE nurse's words, Nancy froze in horror. From her hiding place under the bed she strained to hear the old woman's reply.

"Well, go ahead and search," quavered Mrs Eldridge. "What do I care?"

"You spunky old dear!" Nancy thought.

The nurse snorted. "Hmm, I guess it would be a waste of time! Things are beginning to get on my nerves! You, especially!"

"I'm sorry," Mrs Eldridge said meekly.

"I think you screamed just to make trouble," snapped the nurse, "because you know another patient is due here, and you want to give the place a bad reputation! Well, spare yourself the trouble. The new patient's just telephoned that she will not arrive today."

Nancy nearly groaned. "If someone questions the gate-keeper, I'm sunk!" she thought. "I must get Mrs Eldridge out of here quickly!"

"I'll give you five minutes to eat. Then it'll be nine o'clock. Zero hour for you, old girl. With an ugly laugh, the nurse stamped out of the room.

Nancy waited until the sound of her footsteps had died away before she crept from her hiding place. Hastily she brushed the dust from her black clothing.

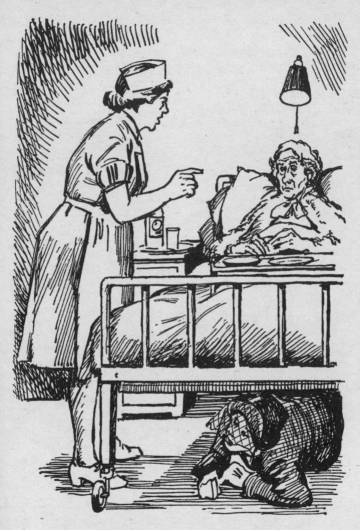

*From her hiding-place, Nancy strained to hear
Mrs Eldridge's reply*

"You were wonderful, Mrs Eldridge!" she whispered. "Now we must work fast and quietly. Can you walk?"

"Yes. They keep us confined to wheel-chairs to weaken us, but I'm still pretty spry. I walk up and down this room for a little exercise. Once I tried to climb out of a ground-floor window, but the creepers pulled loose and I fell and dislocated my shoulder."

"Is that how it happened?" Nancy marvelled at the elderly woman's courage.

While Mrs Eldridge talked, Nancy had taken off her long coat, hat, and gloves. Now she helped the woman to put on her own shoes and Nancy's costume. As she did so, the excited old lady looked at the supper tray.

"Food is cooked with drugs to keep us drowsy all the time," she said. "I eat as little of it as possible."

"How dreadful!" Nancy murmured as she helped her to the door.

"Don't take the main stairs," Mrs Eldridge whispered. "There is a service flight at the rear end of the hall."

"Yes. I explored this place in the dark until they took to locking me in at night. By the way, how could you open my door?"

"I'll tell you later," said Nancy. "Come now."

The service stairway was a steep flight of enclosed steps which Mrs Eldridge had to go down sideways, one at a time.

With maddening slowness, they reached the first floor and saw lights reflected under the door leading to the hall. The stairs squeaked and Nancy's nerves grew tenser. Near the ground floor the staircase divided and Mrs Eldridge said they should take the left branch.

"The other leads into the kitchen. This one takes you to the cellar landing and the entrance into the garden," she whispered.

A few minutes later they stepped into the open air. As fast as Mrs Eldridge could go, the two hastened to the car. Nancy's heart leaped with joy when she saw its hulking shadow amongst the trees.

"Bess!" she whispered. "Any trouble?"

"No, but I thought you'd never come! Bess choked back tears of relief as she and Nancy helped Mrs Eldridge into the back of the car.

"You'll have to sit on the floor, and keep your head down," Nancy warned Mrs Eldridge. "Go now, Bess. Good luck!

"Oh, Nancy, aren't you coming?" Bess whispered.

"No, I have work to do here."

"Well, for goodness sake, be careful!"

The car moved out of the shadows to the driveway. Nancy followed and watched the red rear-lights proceed towards the closed gate.

"Oh, I hope there'll be no trouble," she thought The watchman came out with a torch and shone it into Bess's window as she stopped. The dog began to bark frantically.

For what seemed an age, the gate-keeper held the light in Bess's face and Nancy heard him talking, but could not make out the words. *What was the trouble?*

At last he shrugged, opened the gate, and the car shot through. As the rear-lights disappeared down the lane, Nancy gave sigh of relief.

"Now to send Ned the alarm!"

As she turned back towards the house, Nancy saw that it was ablaze with lights. Figures darted back and forth across the illuminated windows. Reaching the mansion, Nancy concealed herself in the shrubbery alongside a wall. A window above her was suddenly flung open, and Bell's voice rang out.

"Emily, your carelessness is inexcusable!" he thundered. "I am not afraid of the old crone's escaping, but she will give us a pretty hour's work searching the grounds."

"Listen, Simon," Miss Tyson replied. "I can't be everywhere at once."

"You can keep your eyes open," he snapped. "Mrs Eldridge smuggled her bracelet to that doctor right under your nose!"

"Forget it," the woman retorted. "You've taken in enough money from these old women. Why don't you quit this business? Then we could all leave for South America as you promised."

"Not with several thousand dollars still to be had," Bell snarled. "See that every shrub and bush in this place is combed for Mrs Eldridge, and when you find her, bring her to me."

"All right."

"We will wring the money out of her tonight!"

Nancy peered upwards. She could see Bell's pointed beard thrust from the window. Suppose he saw her? But after a few moments he withdrew his head.

"So they are searching the grounds," Nancy mused. "In that case, Mrs Eldridge's room would be the safest place for me."

The Great Dane growled menacingly at the gatehouse. Nancy shivered. Suppose they let him loose!

She edged softly to the rear door by which she and the elderly woman had left, and crept up the steep, dark stairs. When she was halfway to the second floor, the door below her was thrown open and a voice asked:

"Has anyone looked in here?"

As light streamed into the stairway, Nancy ran on tiptoe to the top.

"I'll check the third floor," the same woman said.

As she started upwards, Nancy whirled and quietly sprinted up the narrow stairs, two steps in one leap. At the top was a low door. The young detective opened it, stepped into blackness, and closed the door softly behind her. From the musty smell she surmised that it was an attic. For a few moments she listened. Silence. Then came a scurrying noise and a squeak. *Mice!*

Nancy felt along the wall until her fingers found a switch. She flicked it on and a single bulb glowed in the middle of a great raftered room. Here and there stood trunks, barrels, and old furniture. Against one wall rested dozens of dismantled bedsteads.

In the middle a ladder led up to rafters and there Nancy could see a partial floor with boxes and piles of newspapers.

Suddenly she noticed a small, round window at one end of the attic. With a gasp Nancy quickly flicked off the light, hoping no one had seen it from the grounds!

She felt her way to the window and looked down. Several torches were moving near the outbuildings.

"That's where I'll have to go," she said to herself, "in order to send the alarm to Ned. I must reach the pigeon loft unseen."

Just then she heard a low sigh behind her in the dark attic. It seemed to come from above. "Who could be hiding here? Or maybe it's a prisoner. Morgan!" she thought. "So this is where they're keeping him."

Nancy felt her way back to the ladder and cautiously climbed part way up.

"Morgan—" she whispered.

There was a gasp. "Yes—who is it?"

"Nancy Drew. Are you well enough to move?"

"No," was the faint reply. "I'm very weak."

Nancy's heart sank. "Never mind," she said encouragingly. "I'm going to get you out of here somehow. Just—"

At that moment footsteps clumped on the attic stairs. Nancy scampered up the ladder and felt amongst the boxes and papers. Just as she crouched down, the light went on.

From a cramped position she saw that Morgan, very pale, lay on a mattress, well-concealed amid the boxes. Scattered at her feet were bits of torn newspaper.

Peering between boxes, she saw two men at the door. One had a thin, pinched face, the other was stout with pale, flabby features.

The big man was puffing. "There's nobody here, Tarr. All those stairs for nothing!"

"Chief said he saw a light."

"Chief's wrong."

The other man sighed. "We'd better search, anyway."

Very cautiously, Nancy tried to relieve her cramped muscles. But just as they walked beneath the platform, her foot slipped, pushing a small piece of paper off the platform. As it fluttered down, the two men looked up.

"Morgan?" Tarr called sharply. "You alone?"

The sick man groaned slightly.

"Forget it," said Jackson. "There's nobody with him. Probably a mouse disturbed the paper. Place is full of 'em."

"We ought to search," the thin man said weakly.

The heavy one grinned craftily. "Let's not, and say we did."

The other gave a weak laugh and they left, flicking out the light.

"I'll be back soon, Morgan," Nancy promised. As quickly as possible she made her way out of the attic down to the second floor.

"I'll wait in Mrs Eldridge's room," Nancy decided. "When I hear the searchers come inside, I'll sneak out to the pigeon loft."

Softly she turned the knob and stepped into the upper hall.

A startled scream rang out.

"Oh—oh—help!" A crash of crockery froze Nancy in her tracks. The nurse's helper was in the hallway, staring at Nancy open-mouthed, a tray of broken dishes at her feet.

Nancy darted past her and ran down the main stairs, while behind her she heard the girl shouting the alarm.

A chorus of excited voices came from the second floor, but Nancy reached the veranda without being seen. She ran along its entire length and dived into the shrubbery, panting. Then, hoping that she would not be seen, Nancy darted across the open lawn to a clump of bushes.

A moment later her heart leaped with alarm. Somewhere nearby she heard the dog sniffing. The next instant the animal broke into frantic barking.

Heavy footsteps raced up and a blinding light focused on Nancy's face.

"Here she is!" a deep voice shouted. "I got her, chief!"

· 18 ·

The Underground Cell

MORE running steps came closer and stopped outside the bushes.

"Come out of there!" ordered a harsh voice.

Nancy's heart sank. The speaker was Adam Thorne! Knowing resistance was futile, she crept from the bushes and stood up in the glare of a powerful torch beam. In the darkness just beyond, Nancy could hear the dog snarling and her captors breathing heavily.

"It isn't the old lady!" came Miss Tyson's voice. "It's Nancy Drew!"

Adam Thorne growled. "*What?* I thought we'd knocked her out of action."

Miss Tyson said in a worried voice, "That's what Tarr and Jackson reported. Tarr himself pushed her—"

"Quiet!" snapped Thorne. "She's tricked us. Take her to the house. We'll lock her up."

Quick as lightning, Nancy plunged out of the light and desperately raced down the hill. Taken by surprise, her captors hesitated, then pounded after her, the dog barking furiously.

Blinded by the sudden change from light to darkness, Nancy stumbled and fell. An instant later the Great Dane leaped on her.

"Grab that leash!" shouted Thorne. The dog was

yanked back, then someone jerked Nancy to her feet.

"We'll take her to the house!" panted Thorne.

With the ex-lawyer in the lead, flanked by the nurse and the attendant, and guarded in the rear by the gate-keeper and his dog, Nancy was marched to the mansion. Bell was waiting in the main hall.

"Who is this?" he demanded. "Where's Mrs Eldridge?"

"We haven't found the old fox yet," Thorne answered. "This is the Drew girl I warned you about."

Bell's eyes narrowed. "What do you mean by trespassing on private property?"

"I meant no harm," Nancy replied truthfully.

Thorne snorted scornfully. "She's been spying. It's your fault, Bell. I told you not to bring Dr Spire here. If the old woman's shoulder was dislocated, you should have let it stay that way. Too bad you aren't a real doctor," he added unpleasantly. "You could have set it yourself."

"Never mind that," Miss Tyson put in sharply. "How did she get in here?"

"Luther, bring the gate-keeper quickly!" Bell ordered. "Just how did you get in, Miss Drew?"

"I came in at the entrance," Nancy replied. "The larkspur is beautiful—"

"I'm not interested in flowers. I think—" Bell checked himself.

He turned to Adam Thorne and spoke in an undertone, but Nancy, straining her ears, heard him say "password to Larkspur Lane" before their voices became hushed.

After a few minutes the attendant appeared with the

gateman. "Jones, have you ever seen this young woman?" Bell demanded, glaring at the man standing before him.

"I? No, sir," the guard declared, not recognizing Nancy dressed in her own clothes.

"Did anybody come in by the gate tonight?" Bell asked sharply.

Nancy saw fear flicker in the man's eyes as he met Bell's hard stare. Through no fault of his own, the gateman had let intruders into the grounds!

Jones swallowed. "Uh—no, chief," he said. "Nobody came in or out."

A wave of relief swept over Nancy. No alarm would go out for Mrs Eldridge. The gang would continue to think she was hiding in the grounds.

"All right," Bell said. "Get back to the gate." Then, turning to Thorne, he said, "Let's continue this in my office."

Miss Tyson grinned maliciously as she prodded Nancy along and into a large, luxurious room. A thick green carpet covered the floor and in the centre stood a large mahogany desk. The walls, panelled in a rich-looking wood, were hung with costly oil paintings.

"Shut the door, Luther," Bell ordered.

Bell seated himself behind the desk, motioning Nancy to stand opposite him. There was tense silence for a moment. Then Bell reached for a desk telephone.

"I am going to call the police, Miss Drew, and turn you over to them on a charge of trespassing, breaking, and entering with intent to steal."

"I wish you would," Nancy replied, "if it is possible over that dummy telephone."

"Didn't I tell you she was sharp-eyed?" Thorne

scolded. "You can't fool her. Follow my advice and put her away. This is a waste of time."

"What do you mean? Do you wish to have me summon the police?" Bell blustered. "Why do you call this a dummy telephone?"

"Because, in answer to your first question, I should be happy to be escorted from here under police protection," Nancy retorted. "I know the telephone is a dummy because there are no—"

She checked herself abruptly. No use proving her powers of observation!

"See here, Nancy Drew," Bell said, pointing a finger at her. "Stop all this talk and tell me how you entered these grounds—and why. I know all about you. Sylvan Lake is a long distance from here, and you did not walk."

"There are various ways of travelling."

"Bell, I'm telling you it's just foolishness to try to match wits with this girl," Thorne put in. "I know a way to make her talk—and what's more, I'm sure her illustrious father will pay plenty to get his precious daughter back."

"An excellent idea, Thorne," Bell said with an evil smile. "What would you suggest we do first?"

"Put her in the cistern," said Thorne. "I guess a couple of days without food or drink, down in the dark and cold with the rats and spiders, will make Miss Drew answer any questions we ask."

Miss Tyson laughed harshly, looking straight at Nancy to see if she winced at the prospect. "That will take some of the snap out of her," she said.

A shiver went down Nancy's spine, but she did not change expression.

Bell's cold eyes studied her carefully. "You've caused us a lot of trouble," he said softly. "Because of you we had to give up our other headquarters. My partner Mr Tooker will not overlook that very readily." Bell toyed with a sharp-pointed letter opener on his desk.

Miss Tyson spoke up. "The pigeon keeper guessed she had found that bird, kept it, and then followed it to Tooker's. Now I'm sure he was right. Only from the message that pigeon carried could she have learned the password. And I still say she couldn't have entered without it."

Luther cleared his throat. "But Jones said—"

"He was lying," Miss Tyson broke in. "Where's the car you came in?" she asked Nancy.

Nancy thought it best to keep stalling. The farther away Bess, George, and Mrs Eldridge got, the safer they would be.

Nancy smiled. "Why don't you search the grounds for the car?"

"That's enough!" snapped Bell. "Take her away."

Nancy knew she was in a hopeless predicament, and reasoned that more was to be gained by strategy than by a desperate attempt to break loose. As she was marched out of the room, she heard Bell say, "The disappearance of the Eldridge woman and the Drew girl showing up have me so upset I can't think. I'm going upstairs and tell Adolf. Let him handle this. It's dynamite."

"Do as you please," Thorne said coldly.

Nancy, her arms pinned behind her back, was shoved out on to the porch and towards the buildings beyond the house. Just outside the pigeon loft, Thorne stooped and jerked at an iron ring in the ground. It was

attached to a round steel lid about three feet in dia-
meter. Beneath it gaped a black hole.

"Well, down you go, Nancy Drew!" Thorne
laughed.

Nancy looked round desperately. There was no
escape. As the nurse pushed her, the trapped girl was
forced to start down a swaying, flimsy wooden ladder
into the dark, damp hole. Down, down, ten or twelve
feet Nancy went, until she could feel the slimy bottom
under her feet.

"This is worse than I bargained for," she thought
ruefully.

The ladder was jerked up and Thorne called, "Don't
worry. You may have it back."

There was a series of splitting noises, and pieces of
the ladder came raining down around Nancy's head.
As she threw up her arms to protect herself, she heard
Thorne laugh sardonically.

Then the lid clanged shut!

· 19 ·

Caught!

DESPAIR filled Nancy's heart and she shivered. The dampness of the old cistern covered her like a clammy hand.

She took a deep breath. "Come on now," Nancy scolded herself. "Brace up and try to find a way out!"

Stretching her arms wide, Nancy could feel nothing, so she knew her prison was wider than its three-foot lid. When her eyes became accustomed to the darkness, she noticed tiny gleams of light coming from above. Perhaps the lid did not fit tightly.

"Or maybe it's a phosphorescent glow from some decaying thing," Nancy thought with distaste. "Whatever it is, I must find out."

Balancing herself with outstretched arms, she walked cautiously across the slippery floor. It was uneven and Nancy stepped ankle-deep in cold water. A moment later her fingers brushed the moist stone wall. She stared upwards and saw light coming through chinks in the wall directly above her.

"I must try to reach those openings, but how?" Then Nancy remembered the pieces of ladder Thorne had mockingly thrown to her.

"Maybe I can use them after all," she thought. Repressing a shudder, Nancy slid her fingers over the slimy floor for the fragments. "Now's no time to be squeamish."

Finding a piece of wood, Nancy fingered it anxiously for a nail. Feeling one, she pulled it loose from the rotten wood and noted that it was long and strong.

"Maybe this will work, and maybe it won't," she said half-aloud.

To her horror, she was answered by a throaty chuckle. Nancy gasped. As the sound was repeated she dropped the nail, unnerved. Then, fighting for control, the desperate girl located the noise—it was coming from above. Was someone watching through the chinks?

"*Kel—ek—koo—oo—oo!*" As the new noise blended with the chuckles, Nancy suddenly grinned in relief.

"Pigeons! The light must be coming from the loft!"

Frantically she sought the lost nail. Locating it, Nancy began to dig vigorously at the loose mortar. Soon she had hollowed out space enough to give herself one toehold. A little farther above, Nancy dug again, and repeated the process until she could reach no higher on the wall.

Then she climbed up and chipped out another hold. The mortar was hard and her fingers, clutching the nail, grew cramped. The higher she went, the more difficult the task became.

Finally the imprisoned girl was forced to cling to the damp wall, her toes and the fingers of one hand digging into the niches she had scooped out. With her free hand she scraped a higher grip for herself.

At last Nancy's fingers found the openings through which the light filtered. A big stone rocked under her hand!

Mingled excitement and alarm shot through her Here was the way out! "But suppose I can't move the stone or I fall!" she thought. About eight feet below was the stone floor of the cistern.

Nevertheless, Nancy forced herself to try pushing the stone aside. She failed, but suddenly it came loose and fell inwards over her head. As the stone plummeted down, it grazed her shoulder, but Nancy managed to grab the top edge of the hole and hold tight.

With a sigh of relief she pulled herself through the enlarged opening and up to freedom! On the earthen floor of the pigeon loft, the young sleuth fell back exhausted and closed her eyes. A few moments later she opened them to the sound of fluttering wings and sleepy cooing. The loft was lit by a large bright bulb under a small cage containing a pigeon.

"This is the sick bird," Nancy conjectured, "and it is being kept warm."

Capsules for messages lay on a shelf. "Good," Nancy thought. She took a pencil and small pad from her blouse pocket and wrote three identical messages: "SP at once". Nancy inserted them in the capsules, then caught a pigeon and attached the capsule to its anklet. Quickly she caught another bird, then a third.

"I'd better turn out the light for a few minutes so I won't be seen releasing these pigeons," she decided, and unscrewed the bulb.

Nancy now felt her way to the door, opened it, and released the birds, "Fly straight to Ned," she muttered. "He's waiting at the Tooker estate."

Hoping no one had seen the light go off, Nancy replaced the bulb again and fled from the coop to the carriage-house garage.

Here she considered her next move. Nancy knew there must be lights on the landing field, because the gang used their plane at night. "But how do they turn them on? Perhaps at a switchbox in here?"

She opened the door wide enough to squeeze through and saw two large saloons. One was the old car used to kidnap Dr Spire. Walking past it, Nancy glanced inside and stopped short. She had glimpsed a white blur! Was it a face she saw?

Nancy turned quietly and stepped nearer. As she stared, a figure in one corner of the back seat moved. Someone was seated there, bound and gagged. Quickly Nancy opened the car door. Removing the gag, she asked, "Morgan, how did you get here?"

"They brought me down," he said hoarsely. "Thorne's going to finish me off to keep me from talking. But they'll do it where no one will find me." He breathed heavily. "The gang's ready to escape. Tooker has given the signal to clear out."

"How soon?" asked Nancy as she quickly worked at his bonds.

"I don't know," he whispered. "Soon."

"What about the patients?"

"They'll herd 'em into the cellar." Anger gave the weakened man strength to continue. "The gang isn't worried about them. They figure the shock'll kill some of the old ladies and the rest'll be too confused and terrified to be of much help to the police."

"Those men are brutes!" Nancy exclaimed. "They mustn't get away!"

Quickly she climbed from the car and took the nail from her pocket. Nancy inserted it into a tyre valve, holding it open until all the air had hissed out. She did the same to the rest of the tyres on both cars, then hurried back to Morgan.

"Do you know how they turn on the landing-field lights?" she asked.

"Big oak," he said weakly, "at the edge of the field. Switch box nailed to the tree."

"I must turn them on," she said. "I'll be back!"

Nancy dashed from the garage and ran down the hill towards the level field at the bottom. The moon was coming up and the sloping lawn was bathed in pale light."

"If only they don't see me!"

From somewhere behind Nancy came the deep-throated bark of the Great Dane. Was he loose on the grounds? she wondered.

At one end of the landing field, Nancy could see the plane and at the other a clump of trees. She angled left and raced down towards them.

Reaching the shadow of the trees, she stopped and tried to spot the oak. Again, she heard the dog's bark—this time closer.

Nancy looked back.

The huge beast was silhouetted on the brow of the hill, straining against a leash held by the gate-keeper. He began pulling the man down the slope.

"Does he scent me?" Nancy tried not to think about it, and pressed deeper into the clump of trees.

There was the oak! And gleaming in the moonlight a metal box nailed to the trunk! Nancy darted to it, opened the door, and pulled the single switch inside.

Out on the field, spots of light were coming up through the short grass. "Clever," she thought. "They're sunk in the earth, and aren't noticeable in daylight. Now for the plane!"

The far side of the landing area was bordered by woodland. Nancy ran from her shelter to the woods, then hastened along the edge of the field, keeping within the tree line. At the far end, she crouched low, dashed across the clearing, and crept under the low wing of the small plane.

Nancy knew that the fuel drains were on the underside of the wings. She felt along the surface until her fingers encountered a T-shaped metal valve.

"This must be it," she decided, and pressed upwards. A stream of fuel flowed to the ground! Nancy found that by turning the valve slightly she could lock it open. Then she hurried to the other wing and did the same thing.

"Now," Nancy said to herself, "that should ground the gang! I'll get back to Morgan and hide him before the men go to the cars."

As she started to move, however, Nancy heard the Great Dane growling. Coming down the field were the dog and the gate-keeper, with four men running behind them. Nancy recognized Thorne, Bell, and Luther, but the fourth was a tall stranger. As they drew nearer, she saw he had a gaunt, cruel face, and guessed he was Adolf Tooker.

"I'm telling you I didn't turn on the lights," came Luther's voice.

"Well, somebody did," Thorne growled. "Jones, can't you shut that dog up?"

"There's a prowler down here," replied the gate-man. "That's what's the matter with him."

As the party reached the plane, they stopped less than thirty feet from Nancy. The dog strained towards her hiding-place, whining.

Nancy took a deep breath. "I'm really in a tight spot!" she thought. If she moved from the shadow of the plane's wing, the men would see her. If she didn't, the dog would attack her!

Suddenly shouts came from the hillside and Nancy saw the bobbing rays of torches. "Wait for me!" called Miss Tyson. "Something's gone wrong!" her shrill voice warned.

The tall man said sharply, "Jones, take that dog and find out what the trouble is! We'll search down here for the prowler."

As the gate-keeper pulled the dog away, louder shouts came from the hillside and the four men looked up towards the moving lights.

"It's now or never!" Nancy thought. Crouching low, she ran out on the moonlit field.

The SP

NOT daring to look back, Nancy raced for the shelter of the woods, wondering if she could make it before being detected.

Suddenly she heard a hoarse shout. "Look, chief! There goes a girl!"

The young sleuth's heart sank.

"Catch her!" Thorne yelled.

"No, you fool," barked Bell. "We haven't time! Into the plane, everybody! Go ahead, Adolf!"

"Wait!" came the tall man's hard voice. "I smell petrol."

Thorne gave an angry exclamation and Bell said, "I do, too. Where's it coming from?"

"There's probably a leak in one of the fuel tanks," said Luther. Quickly he ducked under the wing. "One drain valve is open!" he shouted.

"Open?" thundered Bell. "Who did that?"

At once Thorne climbed into the plane. In a moment he gave an angry yell. "We have no fuel!" he cried and jumped out. "The gauges read empty!"

Miss Tyson raced up to them with three men and a girl at her heels, followed by the gate-keeper and his barking dog.

"Everything's gone wrong!" she exclaimed.

At that moment a plane swooped soundlessly out of

the sky. Before it taxied to a full stop, several armed police officers jumped out and surrounded the criminals. A powerful searchlight was turned on the confused gang.

A voice over a loudspeaker ordered, "Stand where you are! No one move!"

"Ned!" Nancy cried out.

She raced from the woods and reached the plane as he leaped from it, followed by Dave, her father, and the pilot.

"Dad!" Nancy exclaimed as Carson Drew caught her up in his arms.

"Are you hurt?" he asked quickly.

"No, Dad, but I'm so glad to see you! Ned, you're just wonderful!"

"Oh, Nancy, you take such chances," he said. "But I was sure happy I could come to the rescue."

In a moment a second noiseless plane skimmed down on to the field. Out jumped Burt, Lieutenant Mulligan, and two members of his detective squad. They joined the others in the circle of light, while the officers began snapping handcuffs on the prisoners.

"Miss Drew," Lieutenant Mulligan said, "Ned Nickerson informed me of your plan and I called the police."

"I'm glad the mystery is solved, Lieutenant," said Nancy, then turned to Thorne. "Where are the old ladies?" she asked anxiously.

The gang members had been staring at Nancy in disbelief. "You!" Thorne spluttered. "How did you get out of the cistern?"

"First answer my question," said Nancy.

"They're in the cellar," Bell replied shortly.

Miss Tyson spoke up. "They are not in the cellar."

As Bell looked at her, puzzled, she added, "I didn't have time to put them there! As soon as I saw the air was out of our car tyres, I knew something had gone wrong with the plans. I wanted to get away—fast!"

"What did you do with Morgan?" Nancy asked quickly.

"Nothing. He's still in the car."

Nancy explained Morgan's condition to the police, who promised that the sick man would be taken to a hospital.

Thorne glared at Nancy. "How did you get out of the cistern?"

"Climbed out," Nancy said directly. "I used the ladder you gave me."

Miss Tyson gasped. "That's impossible."

Briefly, Nancy told how she had escaped and sent for help.

" 'SP at once'," Ned said with a grin. "Sailplane at once!"

"Also, send police," Nancy added.

"These aren't gliders?" Tooker asked.

"No," Ned answered. "They're motorized sail-planes. They were perfect for this job because we flew them here using the motor, then cut it out and landed soundlessly."

He grinned at Dave. "All we had to do was find two sailplanes. We finally rented these from an airport in the next county. The police provided the pilots."

"Dad," said Nancy, "how did you hear about the plan?"

"Ned briefed me. He called our house on the chance that I'd returned from Chicago." Looking at Adam Thorne, Mr Drew added, "I'm proud of my daughter,

Thorne. She planned to take you and your accomplices by surprise, so you couldn't harm the old ladies before you bolted."

Lieutenant Mulligan cleared his throat. "Miss Drew, you're a fine detective."

Nancy smiled and thanked him.

Adolf Tooker turned to Bell and said angrily, "This is the girl you said would be no trouble?"

"I warned Bell about her," Thorne spoke up, "but he wouldn't listen!"

"It's not my fault," said Bell, his voice rising nervously. "It's Thorne's. Ever since he read about the Cornings' jewelled crystal collection he wanted to steal it. Then he dragged us into the scheme and bungled it! My men were doing all his work!

"Whenever I wanted Tarr and Jackson, they were trailing Nancy Drew in the saloon or spying on that Sylvan Lake place. They even set the dog on her. Twice they snatched Morgan, and Jackson showed the blue fire night after night to scare him. It finally worked. Then suddenly Morgan wouldn't go along with us, so we had to teach him a lesson.

"As for Tarr," Bell went on bitterly, "he spent days making the firework wheel and rigging up an asbestos-lined box for it."

Tarr gave a sickly grin. "All I had to do was shut the door of the box and the blue fire was gone—like magic!"

Jackson's face was pale. "We only did what Thorne ordered."

"Be quiet, all of you!" barked Thorne. "Don't you know there are police listening?"

"It doesn't matter," Adolf Tooker said wearily. "They'll find all the evidence they need here."

"Is this your whole gang?" Mulligan asked sharply.

Tooker looked round the group which included the gate-man with the dog, the pigeon-keeper, and the nurse's aide whom Nancy had startled in the hall.

"Yes."

Miss Tyson's assistant was shaking with fright. "I was only doing what Dr Bell ordered. He told me the patients were too nervous to have visitors."

"He's no doctor," Nancy told her. "And I find it hard to believe Miss Tyson is a real nurse."

The hard-faced woman shot her a venomous look.

"The police will find out about them all," Lieutenant Mulligan said grimly.

At that moment two helicopters appeared, lights flashing. They landed on the field and the rotors were silenced.

"Last stage of Nancy's plan," Ned said. "Reinforcements!"

"Okay," called a police officer to the arriving men. "Load this gang in the copters and take 'em away!"

An hour later Nancy had the biggest thrill of the evening. As she walked into the Cornings' living-room with her father and the boys, she saw Mrs Eldridge seated in a big chair with little Marie asleep on her lap. At one side stood the child's mother, on the other a tall stranger.

"Nancy," the old woman said happily, "this is my nephew John. Nancy Drew is the girl who—" Tears filled her eyes and she could not go on.

"Yes," he said, "Nancy Drew has done a wonderful job. Thank you, Nancy."

"The hospital called," said Mrs Corning. "Morgan will be all right! We're so grateful to you for clearing up the mystery about him."

"Will you take him back?" Bess asked.

"Of course. He is honest and faithful. We know his true story. There can't be any more trouble."

Nancy thanked her friends for helping her. She gave Bess and George each a hug and quickly excused herself to change her clothes. When she came downstairs, Mrs Corning had a tray of tempting food waiting.

"Oh good!" said Nancy. "Tea was a long time ago. I'm famished!"

While everyone ate, Mrs Eldridge told what she had learned while a prisoner at Larkspur Lane. Tooker, whose real name was Van Hofwitz, was an international confidence man.

"The hospital was his idea," she said. "He made Bell a partner and he was to pass as a doctor. Thorne had put money into the venture while in prison. As soon as he escaped, he joined the others."

Mrs Eldridge went on to say that Von Hofwitz ingratiated himself into various social circles. He would introduce the fake doctor to wealthy ladies who complained of old age.

"I see now how silly I was," Mrs Eldridge said. "I was taken in by their suave manners and my own vanity."

She revealed that the unscrupulous pair would persuade the women to go secretly to the hospital. There, using drugs and threats, Bell prevailed upon the patients to sign away large parts of their wealth to him.

Mr Drew spoke up. "Thorne is a very sharp lawyer and no doubt the contracts he drew up for you women to sign seemed harmless enough, but could not be changed, even if your relatives tried to break them."

"But your courage, Mrs Eldridge," said Nancy, "helped to put an end to the whole scheme. There are two questions I hope you can answer," she added. "Why did the gang use *blue bells* in the code?"

"Because Bell was so conceited he wanted his own name in it. Blue, of course, was the colour of the flowers growing so profusely round the estate."

"And why was the pigeon released from the plane?"

"Tooker was flying from the mansion to an appointment with an old woman in Pennsylvania that day. He let the bird go on the way so that it would reach his estate more quickly."

"Thank you, Mrs Eldridge, for the answers to my questions," Nancy said. "And now I'll go upstairs and get your bracelet for you."

"No, dear," said the old lady. "I want you to keep it as a memento."

"How wonderful!" Nancy hugged her.

Mr Corning spoke up. "And I am going to order crystal earrings in the form of tiny larkspurs for you and the other girls."

"Oh, how exciting!" Bess exclaimed. "Thank you very much."

George grinned and added her thanks.

Nancy protested that she wanted no reward. "I'm just happy everything turned out right."

Ned grinned. "If I were to give Nancy the reward she'd like best, I'd hand her another mystery to solve. I'll find you a mystery by tomorrow morning," he promised jokingly.

"And I'll be ready for it," Nancy said with a twinkle in her eyes. "But make it very, very complicated and original." *The Bungalow Mystery* proved to be both!